Some Bear to Love

TERRY BOLRYDER

DEDICATION

For my family, who always supports me.

CONTENTS

Acknowledgements

Special thanks to my readers who have been so supportive, my editors, and my friends

CHAPTER 1

Kim Starling didn't know exactly who she was looking at, but she knew that she liked him.

It was only her second day in Grand Cayman. It was sunny and beautiful as usual, the water was a brisk, clear blue-green, and the sand was soft and pale and dotted with tourists enjoying the weather.

Her heightened shifter senses picked up every scent brought to her on the breeze.

Cinnamon, from the morning breakfast buffet, fruit from the same, sunblock and coconut tanning oil, salt and mist from the ocean, something uniquely fishy and fresh from the same.

The raucous shouts around her were loud in her ears but she didn't mind. She liked crowds, liked people. Liked having them around.

She crouched and brushed sand aside and picked up a worn pink shell. She ran her thumb over it as she walked to the dock where the object of her attention was loading a huge sleep-aboard yacht.

It was a tour of the island, and it would be overnight. And it was apparently mandatory, according to her orientation pamphlet that she'd been given for winning the giveaway she couldn't even remember having entered.

In fact, she was sure she hadn't entered, but she was used to shifter families doing weird things to match-make, and that's exactly what she figured this was.

The man on the dock was gorgeous. More than gorgeous. She was just trying to figure out what he was. Bear, probably, from the height and breadth of his shoulders.

He had long, gorgeous blond hair, sun-streaked from life on the island, and bronzed skin that glowed in the sun. And the most striking eyes she'd ever seen, in an intense turquoise shade that perfectly matched the color of the beautiful water around them.

He seemed oblivious to the fact that he was being watched as he loaded and counted the boxes and bags from the dock onto the boat.

He wore a navy blue captain's hat that was probably just to please the tourists, and she had to admit it pleased her just fine.

She folded her arms, chucked the shell to the side, and walked over to his boat.

He didn't notice her at first. He was busy marking things off on a clipboard.

Kim was used to being noticed, though. At 5'10" with mostly bear blood, and long, thick black hair she wore in cornrows that were then tied into a thick braid, with oddly gray eyes, she stood out in a crowd.

She could tell by the set of his shoulders when he sensed her presence, and when he whipped around to look at her, his long ponytail flew in the wind, catching the sunlight in shades of beguiling gold.

A different scent lit the air. One of an alpha male. A strong one, and her body responded immediately.

This was just what she needed.

She stuck out a hand as he rose to his full height and looked down at her with folded arms. "My name is Kim Starling. I'll be on the boat with you today."

"I know who you are," he said flatly, looking down at her hand but not taking it. "And just so you know, I'm not looking for a mate."

She frowned. "Don't get ahead of yourself, friend. Who said I was either?"

He pursed full lips and that aqua gaze studied her. "I have a ship to run. I'm not an idiot to my father's machinations, but I don't have time to watch an alpha female while I have a crew to manage and a ship to pilot."

Footsteps jogged up behind them on the dock, and they both whipped around to see the newcomer.

It was a younger-looking skipper and he tipped his

hat to the captain. "My first time navigating! Amazing right? When Sam told me…"

A wide grin spread across her face at the dismay on the captain's face at being displaced.

"What do you mean?" he asked, pinning the other with a glare.

"Well, I—I—he wants you to stay on as first mate, but he wants me to take the bulk of the duties."

"Of course he does," the taller man said through gritted teeth. Then he pinned her with a glare that said this was all her fault.

It wasn't of course. It was Sam's fault, whoever that was. But she couldn't say she was sorry that this stunning man now had no excuse to avoid her.

"Well, I'm Kim Starling," she said, shaking the younger man's hand vigorously. "And you are?"

He looked up at her and a blush travelled up his pale skin. "Bart, miss. Born and raised here."

She bent slightly to be at his level, because he was

quite short, despite probably being in his mid-twenties. "Well, then I guess you'll be an excellent pilot and guide on this trip."

"Captain," the taller man drawled. "He'll be an excellent captain." He turned his back on them and strode toward the hotel.

"Then why do you look so pissed about it?" she called out.

He just gave her a glare over his shoulder and stormed off in the direction of the hotel.

She shrugged at the nervous looking Bart who had taken his position. "I'm sorry about that."

"That's just Sebastien's way, ma'am," he said. "He doesn't like not being in control. But Sam said it's time I learn to handle a boat of my own, so we can have two going at once."

"That makes very good sense," she said, putting an arm around his shoulders and making him blush once again. "Now, why don't we head into this ship and you can show me around?"

"I better finish loading the dock, miss."

She eyed the boxes Sebastien had left behind. "All right, but I'll help."

"I really couldn't let you," he said guiltily.

She swept up two large boxes in her strong arms and vaulted up the ramp and into the ship. "Too late!" She stuck her tongue out at him, lowered the boxes into the pile Sebastien had been building.

Then she looked back up at the hotel, for any glimpse of the man that was already starting to take up all of her waking hours.

She couldn't really promise herself to any one man right now, but she couldn't get those particular aqua blue eyes out of her mind.

***

Sebastien Weston thumped heavily on the door to his

father's suite. The old man was in there, he just knew it, and he needed to answer for what he'd done in taking Sebastien's ship from him and giving it to someone who barely knew what they were doing.

His father's matchmaking shenanigans had gone far enough.

"I know you're in there, you old shark!" he shouted. "Give me my boat back."

The door finally swung open, and his father stood behind it, looking tired. Now that he had Sebastien's brother Scott running most aspects of the hotel, his father was free to spend his time sleeping late and micromanaging his sons lives. He knew the old coot wanted grandchildren, but this was far enough.

His father ran his hand through his short, blonde hair shot through with gray and white and yawned. "Bart is fully capable, as you well know. He's been around the ships since he was little, and he has had an excellent teacher." He gestured to his son but Sebastien was not mollified by the compliment. He pushed past his father and strode into the room to pace in front of the sliding glass door that overlooked the ocean below.

He wanted to be out on it, focused on running things, not relegated to interacting with the crew. Especially one bossy, overly talkative she-bear that seemed hungry for a mate.

Well, she was barking up the wrong tree if she thought that was Sebastien. Sure, she was mouthwatering. She seemed strong in a way few people were, and there was a light in her vivacious gray eyes that told him life with her would always be an adventure.

But at the same time, his mate was the sea and his ship and his plans, and he'd never need a woman. They were unnecessary things that just slowed you down. And besides, he had two other brothers who would probably happily find mates.

He paced and grumbled and his father simply laughed aggravatingly and sat in a chair to watch him. Then checked his watch.

"You know, you better get down there if you don't want them to leave without you."

Sebastien flashed angry eyes at his father. "You know damn well they won't leave without me. And I'm not going back down there until you put me back in charge."

"You need to relax," his father said, reclining in the chair and propping his feet on a cushioned ottoman. "All the time it's work work work. It's time you found a mate."

Sebastien narrowed his eyes at his dad. "I knew that's why you brought them here. Giveaway my ass."

"Stop being grumpy. Ladies don't like grumpy men."

Sebastien let out a growl. "I don't care what they like. I'm not taking a mate. You can find your grandchildren elsewhere, crazy old man." He continued to pace. What to do? Already the ship was calling him back. He longed to be on the ocean, his hand on the wheel and the throttle, radio crackling beside him.

He didn't want to be the one herding the passengers, though it would be a small group, since this was an overnight trip and could only house as many as there were cabins for.

Which was even worse. It just made it all the more likely that he'd have to spend time with that treacherous Kim Starling. He didn't need his shifter body reacting to pheromones when he knew logically that that would never be the right thing for him.

A quick roll in the hay, sure. Maybe some hot sex under the island stars. But not mating, and that was surely what a pureblooded shifter like Kim would be wanting.

That would be why his dad had selected her probably.

He wondered what she was exactly. Probably some bear, because of her height. Maybe some grizzly or Kodiac blood.

But there was something else. He could see it in her gray eyes.

Something in him reacted as those gray eyes flashed in his mind, but he tried to ignore it. That was ridiculous. He shook his head and continued to pace, but looked down at the boat when he heard a loud bell ringing, announcing that they would take off soon.

"Looks like they might call your bluff after all," his

dad said, looking highly amused.

Rage burned in Sebastien but he didn't make any move to leave. They wouldn't leave without him. They couldn't.

"You know, it won't be so bad. Perhaps you could just get to know the lady. Be friends."

Ha! She wasn't the type you made friends with. She was the type you had hot sex with under a pier. The type you laughed with under the stars after a passionate kiss. The type you did water sports with and swam with and fell in love with and stayed forever with.

She was not for him.

"I can see how conflicted you are on your face," his dad said sardonically. "Why don't you just go down there and give it a chance? Heck, maybe she's looking for whatever you are. Maybe she doesn't want a commitment."

A shifter female who didn't want a pure-blooded polar bear for a mate? Ha, that didn't exist. He knew that from the many women his father had thrown at him over the years. All of those attempts had seemed half-serious though compared to this latest one. He'd actually brought three women out, one for each of his sons.

It was insane.

He should feel bad for the women, but they did get a free vacation out of the entire thing, not to mention a chance to ensnare very eligible men.

"Ah, looks like your lady friend is going to be first mate, because if I'm not mistaken, your ship just took off without you."

His eyes went wide and he grabbed a pair of binoculars that rested on a nearby table and ran out onto the desk. Sure enough, the boat was leaving, and there was that aggravating tall female with those long, luscious braids out on the top deck with Bart.

Rage sizzled through him. He'd go out, get back aboard his boat, and then have a strongly worded conversation with the woman about just who would be running things. Yes, he thought, rolling up his sleeves as he went. That would make him feel much better.

CHAPTER 2

Kim frowned at the man piloting the small motor boat out to them.

Bart turned to her with sweat on his brow, looking terrified at what the two of them were about to face. But Kim didn't think the whole thing should be delayed by an entitled man who thought the world obviously revolved around him.

They had a captain, the rest of the guests were there, they had a right to leave. In fact, she'd insisted on it. She'd figured that would draw the gorgeous man out when nothing else had seemed to work.

And she'd been right. But she hadn't expected him to

look this angry, standing tall and making the little motor boat he was piloting look tiny in comparison.

As the little craft beat upon the waves, he was barely jarred, and as his ponytail whipped behind him in the wind, and he pinned those icy blue eyes on her even at a distance, a chill ran through her.

She had the sudden urge to run and not face what she'd done, but that wasn't an option. They were on a boat in the middle of the ocean, and it'd be kind of a swim back to the dock. Plus, the man would probably follow her around in that dinghy trying to run her over.

She took a step back and looked at Bart, the captain. "Um, might be a good time to show me to my room."

"I can't, miss, I'm driving."

"Right, totally," she said. "Um, I'll just see which one isn't taken."

"Wait—" he said, obviously wanting her to stay and take some of the blame. But as the tall, angry-looking man got closer she found her bravery fleeing. At least he seemed to be Bart's friend and acquaintance.

He'd seemed to hate her from the moment he met her. She quickly disappeared below deck to the cabins with the bedrooms. There were four, not including the crew quarters upstairs.

As she walked to her cabin, she bumped into something hard and pleasant, and looked up into the eyes of a nice-looking man who must also be a tourist here.

He was tall, taller than her anyway. Slim but muscled, with a nice, light-pink linen shirt, wavy dark hair, pale but smooth skin, and kind blue eyes.

Then what looked like his wife or girlfriend stepped out from beside him.

Damn, not going to get lucky on this trip, it looked like.

"I'm Trudy, this is my husband Zeke," the woman said.

Kim raised an eyebrow at the passive aggressive warning in the her tone. "Nice to meet you," she said, shaking both of their hands. Sure, the man had given her an appreciative look when they'd bumped into one another, but that was it. Nothing to get snitty over. She wasn't looking to take another woman's man.

Truthfully, she'd just like some alone time with that man who was angrily chasing them down, but that didn't seem likely to happen anytime soon. At least in the way she wanted.

He'd probably want some alone time just to yell at her.

"Um, can we help with something?" Zeke asked in a soft voice. His wife stood behind him. She had fluffy blond hair that was frizzing in the humidity and a pinched little face that would probably be pretty if it didn't look so hateful.

"Just looking for my room."

"They're all small, just find one that isn't taken," a friendly voice said from a cabin on the other side of the cramped hallway.

The interior of the ship had wood panelling and a narrow hallway with two small cabins on either side, which consisted mainly of a small full-sized bed and a tiny closet. The ceiling to floor ratio was about half the size of a normal room.

She looked to the room on her left and decided no one was in it yet. She turned to go get her bags, but then realized she had a chance of seeing grumpy pants if she did.

But wouldn't they have to stop the boat for him to try and board? She'd just have to hurry. She jumped up the steps, shuffled across the deck to her stuff, hauled it over her shoulders, and made the mistake of looking out at the water.

He was much closer. Damn, he was beautiful when he was angry. She jumped back down and went into her room, sighing when the door was shut. She set down her bags and opened the tiny window that looked out so the sea breeze could come in and cool her off. Too much running around in the sun.

Not to mention how hot the ship's captain made her. She was resting on the mattress and removing her tee shirt so she could be just in her tankini top when there was a short knock and then the door opened to her room.

She clutched her shirt to her out of reflex and gasped as a man appeared at the door.

"Excuse me?" she said, sitting up.

He averted his eyes. "Sorry, I didn't think you'd be changing that fast."

She grinned. "Just my swimsuit. But you should knock first, wait, and then open in the future." She should be angrier, but the guy was gorgeous, and he couldn't have thought there was anything to wait for this early on in the trip.

Plus, he wasn't the ship captain, and that knock had scared her half to death making her think it was.

Then man in front of her was tall and blond, but with hair that seemed bleached or highlighted to be so. He was muscled, but more the top heavy type that she associated with men who spent all their time in the gym. He wore a skin tight sports shirt and seemed proud of the way his pecs strained against it, making his nipples visible.

He had a square-cut, handsome face that she would have taken more seriously if she hadn't had the captain to compare him to. He was like a sirloin when she was still hoping for some filet mignon.

When the filet calmed down, that is.

Shit, the boat was stopping. She braced a hand on the doorway and stumbled as the boat lurched and lunged against the ocean waves as it slowed.

The man at the doorway reached forward to catch her and she felt her face erupt in a blush as she was pressed up against him.

"Least I can do after walking in on you," he said.

She grinned. "What's your name?" She was in a tankini top that bared her shoulders, generous cleavage, and arms, but didn't feel self conscious at all. She was a woman who loved life, and that included eating lots of good food, having fun, and flaunting what you got.

"Wilson," he said. "And you're Kim?"

"How'd you know?" she asked, looking up into his eyes.

"Actually, I noticed you earlier this week, when you

checked in. I actually came on the boat hoping to meet you."

She swallowed. That was a little weird, right? Feeling odd about it, she pushed out of his arms and looked him up and down. She didn't think there was anything off about him, but that was a little stalkerish.

But she had bigger problems to deal with. She could hear angry shouting from above deck and winced. The 'captain' would be coming aboard soon, presumably taking the last cabin.

That's if he didn't throw her overboard first.

"What's wrong?" Wilson asked, looking concerned. His eyes were a dull olive green color. If he thought to protect her from the monster that was coming, he'd better think again. Wilson was well-muscled and a few inches over six feet, but the man coming after her was about 6'6", well over Wilson's height, and heavily muscled from head to toe. Not to mention intimidating as hell.

"Um, if you don't mind, I think I'll finish changing.

Looks like a good time for a swim, right? No, maybe I'll take a nap. Yes, tell the captain that."

Wilson opened his mouth to ask a question but she shoved him out the door and slammed it behind him, doing the flimsy lock that she didn't think would hold. It was just a little switch you turned that turned a tiny hook inside the door to hold it to the other side. More a way of keeping it closed than locking it.

She heard a series of bumps and cursing upstairs and then the unmistakable voice of the captain. Well, he wasn't the captain anymore. Just Sebastien. It'd be hard to get used to that since she'd been calling him the captain in her head since the first time she'd seen him docking his boat from the balcony of her suite.

She heard Sebastien's angry voice getting louder.

"Where is she?" he boomed out. "Bring her out here. Wait, is she below deck? I'll go get her."

It was more words than she'd heard from him probably since she'd met him. At least, more words about her. Hey, at least she was finally worthy of his notice. She winced at the attention-seeking part of her that was glad he was noticing her at all.

She put her back to the door, trying to hold it closed. She really didn't want to have to face him while he was still angry. She liked riling people up, but she didn't like dealing with them afterwards.

She heard his heavy footsteps clambering down into the cabin and gulped.

"Is this her room? No? This one?" his voice boomed. It was loud, more assertive than she would have guessed from their interaction before.

"Kim?" he asked, knocking. "Get out here."

"No," she called back. "I'm changing." She heard a frustrated huff and murmurs from the others in the hallway.

"I don't have time to deal with you now. I need to make sure Bart is on schedule and deal with him for being insubordinate. But make no mistake, we will deal with this later."

And then his footsteps faded away in a huff. She sighed and relaxed against the door, then realized he had said he was going to go take it out on Bart. She couldn't allow that, not when it was all her fault completely.

She quickly pulled off her pants, leaving her bikini bottoms on and tying a black sarong around her waist for coverage. It was getting hot out there.

She put on flip flops, opened her door, peeked out and saw no one was in the hall. They all must be in their rooms. She heard the captain's, no Sebastien's voice and walked upstairs cautiously, keeping an eye out for him.

Sure enough, he was arguing angrily with Bart, who was trying lamely to defend himself.

"It's my fault," she said, walking up to him with folded arms. She was a good deal taller than Bart, but nowhere near as tall as Sebastien.

Sweat dotted his brow and a few strands of his hair clung to the sides of his face. He'd clearly had to run to catch a boat to get to them, and he wasn't happy about it. He was wearing a white shirt that was much too hot for this, and his captain's hat was nowhere to be seen, leaving his ponytail to whip in the wind, the only cooling element around.

He studied her, a muscle twitching in his taut jaw. He had an angular face, a long jaw leading to a sharp chin with a slight divot in the middle. A sharp, straight nose, high brows and cheekbones, and full lips with a slight pout to them. Though that could have been because he was angry. He was deeply tanned and she found herself wondering if the tan went under his clothes.

She grinned at the thought of finding out.

"You're thinking something dirty, aren't you?" he asked, his anger turning to a smirk. "One track mind. Well, you got Bart here in trouble."

"You're not the captain," she said. "He is."

"Right, but he's not supposed to leave without a first mate." He stared her down, folding his arms to mirror her pose. She could intimidate a lot of people but not him.

He looked down at her. "Nice view," he said

sardonically.

She flushed, looking down at her bikini top, which flashed liberal cleavage. "Thanks," she said. "Same to you." His shirt was slightly open at the front, revealing cut, muscled pecs.

His mouth twitched, but he turned away. "You put everyone in danger. If something had happened to the primary staff member, what would you have done?"

"I can drive a boat," she blurted out, then wished she hadn't. That was a total lie, and she didn't know what had driven her to say it.

"If you don't mind, you can take the helm and I'm going downstairs to check on the passengers," Bart said, probably hoping to take advantage of Sebastien's attention being elsewhere.

"Stop right there," Kim and Sebastien said at the same time. They looked at each other and a stream of electricity sparked between them. They were both incredibly strong willed people, both used to getting people to give them their way. They were flint and stone, and so it seemed inevitable that they'd spark together.

"If you're going to be captain, you stay at the helm," Sebastien said to Bart, keeping his eyes on Kim.

His eyes were the color of the ocean behind him. A vibrant mix of blue and green, but lighter. Sparkling with some unknown emotion. His hair whipped behind him in the air and she longed to reach up, wind that ponytail around her fist, and pull him in.

He took in a sharp breath, as if he could sense her intentions, and then wheeled away from her, heading to the back of the ship. "Come here. Now."

The authoritative tone in his voice made her knees weak, and she followed him away from Bart to where no one could hear them. The ship was long, probably about 50 feet or more, and with the breeze flying past them as the ship cruised forward, she knew their conversation wouldn't carry on the air.

But either way, she wouldn't let him chide her like a child. She faced him with folded arms and a thrust out chest. His eyes moved over her, catching at her hips where her sarong was whipping wildly, threatening to blow away.

He reached for it and she let out a little gasp, but all he did was tie it deftly, his rough fingers brushing against hers. The knot he tied look intricate.

He grinned at her and the effect was unexpected. He had beautiful, straight teeth, but his smile was crooked, wicked. Standing there on the deck with no jacket and his white shirt whipping in the wind and his khakis rolled up, he looked every bit the pirate of her dreams.

He bit his lip as he tilted his head and looked her over again, and then seemed to remember he should be angry.

He took a step forward, backing her against the rail. "You shouldn't have hijacked my boat, princess." He put a hand on either side of her, caging her, making her feel small in the most delicious way, reading to yield to his superior strength and bend to his every whim. "You should be punished."

She raised her eyes sultrily and pushed her boobs a little closer together. "Yes, I probably should. I was a very bad girl." She grinned up at him as his intense eyes focused in on her mouth. He got even closer, nearly pressing against her. He bent down, so that his lips were just a hair's width away.

"You'll have to…swab the deck."

"I have to…what?" She pushed him and he walked away, laughing, hands behind his head. "Excuse me?"

He laughed again. It was a mean sound. At least, it was to her, after he'd left her so completely disappointed. Just one kiss from those perfect lips, and she felt like she probably could have been satisfied forever.

Just one kiss from a hot pirate.

Breeze came in a gust as they changed directions slightly and she caught his scent. He smelled like ocean, plus lilies, plus sand after a storm. She wanted to breath it forever.

She leaned back against the railing, eyes closed.

"Remember, princess," he said. "My boat, my rules. I may not be captain, but I'm still first mate."

She nodded, still enjoying his scent. It was so alpha, so intoxicating. First mate? She wanted him to be *her* mate. She wanted to make him mad against just to feel him close, threatening. She knew that he was a good person, the type who could never really hurt her.

But there was a harshness to him she found sexy. An element of danger. He didn't let anyone fuck with him, and she knew he'd probably make an awesome protector.

She wished briefly that she could have a chance at something like that.

"Hey," he said, and she opened her eyes to see him looking at her with a worried expression. "You're leaning back too far. Don't—"

She startled and looked behind her, catching herself on the railing before she could lose her balance. "Phew, that was close."

He shook his head in a huff, making all of that beautiful golden hair dance around him in the wind. "Don't you even have the slightest bit of self preservation?" He eyed the railing next to her and then put a hand out as he walked forward. "You better come forward." He looked up ahead of the bow of the boat. "There are some waves coming from another boat's wake. You shouldn't be by the edge. One good bump and—".

She rolled her eyes and stayed where she was. Her knees were so weak from his pheromones and him being so close that he didn't think she could move if she wanted to. Besides, did he really think she was the kind of ninny that would—

BUMP. The boat rolled, hard, and then made a thump as it went down. She held on tight, screamed only a little bit, and then righted herself.

His eyes were wide, and then angry but relieved as she settled back against the rail. "Don't take your hands off the—"

"I'm not as stupid as you seem to think I am," she said, waving her hands at him. "Mister—"

She didn't get a change to finish because a huge wave hit, and with a roll and a thump, the boat shuddered beneath her, she slipped off her feet, and went tumbling back over the railing.

The last thing she saw before falling was his angry blue gaze as he lunged to catch her.

She had a brief second to anticipate the landing. This was gonna hurt.

CHAPTER 3

The little—! He guessed he was the only person around who could probably call her little, but just once he wished the frustrating woman would take his advice on something, he thought as he swiped the rescue ring and yelled for Bart to stop the boat. He didn't even think about it, just jumped off the back of the boat into the water to find her.

Luckily, Bart had slowed their speed when he saw the boat wake they were about to hit, so her impact wouldn't hurt as much as it would have if they were going full speed and the water was harder.

Still, he braced for impact, knowing it was going to sting, and needing to get to her as soon as possible. He din't know how good she was at swimming.

The water slapped him as he entered, tucked so as to not go too deep. He surfaced quickly and whipped his hair out of his face, looking for her.

She was sputtering a ways away, since she had flown off the boat before he'd gotten off. She seemed to be able to tread water, and his heart finally stopped trying to pound out of his chest when he realized she was going to be okay.

They both were.

As he swam to her, the rescue ring over one shoulder, it occurred to him that he'd never been this tense, this worked up, this…scared, as he'd been when she'd looked at him with shock and regret in those wild, beautiful gray eyes before she'd gone overboard.

Nothing in his life had ever affected him like this. Over the years he'd grown cold, methodical. But ever since she'd walked onto that dock, she'd been turning things upside down.

He swam forward with sure, quick strokes, and when

he reached her she locked her arms around him, gasping. He had to admit, he liked it. He liked the way she clung to him, liked the way her body felt in the cool water. Liked knowing she was safe.

He had no right to feel that way, but he did. He handed her the safety ring and started pulling them toward the boat.

"I had no idea," she gasped. "What on earth were you thinking backing me up against that rail if it could be so dangerous?"

"Well," he said hoarsely, trying to swim and talk at the same time as he cut his way through the rising and falling swells left behind by the boat. "I'm not used to customers sailing off with my boat. So I don't usually have to call them topside to yell at them. And then usually, if I tell them to hold on to the rail, I don't expect them to do the opposite and wave their hands like a lunatic."

She grumbled something under her breath but hung on to the safety ring and let him tow her.

"What was that?" he asked.

"Nothing," she said. "Thanks for rescuing me."

A muscle in his jaw twitched. "All part of the job. Now don't sue us."

"I could you know. I'm a lawyer."

He groaned as they were nearly to the boat. "I should have known." They had an audience as he pulled up to the ladder that would pull them onto the lower deck that would lead inside to the cabins. He helped her climb up first. "Nothing to see here folks. Bart, if you could lower the anchor and help people get into their snorkel gear, this is a good place to stop for lunch and a swim if people would like."

He climbed out behind her as she collapsed on the carpeted deck. Rough carpet was necessary or the sun burned the client's feet. He heaved himself out behind her, feeling exhausted as the adrenaline wore off.

But then he looked out at the ocean. Enjoyed the feel of being out here, isolated from land. Rocking gently. There was a lot to be grateful for. They were both okay. He had his ship back, and hopefully after that stunt, the frustrating, beautiful woman next to him wouldn't be doing that again.

"Look," he said, as she stretched her neck and checked her limbs to make sure she was okay. "You might be in charge back in whatever big city you're from. You might be the top in your cycling gym, or whatever." Her body was curvaceous but also fit and muscled, so he knew she worked out. A lot. "But here on the island, dangerous things can happen. You need to learn to take commands."

She grinned, tossing her gorgeous black braids over her shoulder and winking at him mischievously. "I'll take your commands any day, captain," she said. And then before he could stop her, she leaned forward and planted one right on his mouth.

Heat sizzled straight to his groin, and then the kiss was over too quickly, and she was standing and swaying those delectable hips as she walked into the cabin to get dry.

He just sat there for a moment, then raised a hand to touch his lips. He couldn't remember the last time he'd been kissed. No, *he* was the one who did the kissing, he thought indignantly.

But all he could think of was those full lips on his. Those mischievous gray eyes coming closer. His cock hardened and he growled at the thoughts flooding his head. Her in his cabin, her hands tied above her head as she took his every command.

Her screaming his name and calling him captain.

His lips between her legs as she screamed beneath him.

He shook his head. He had a job to do. He'd do it. And he wouldn't succumb to his dad's stupid matchmaking plans. The sea was his mistress, master and wife all in one. He needed nothing more.

Besides, things should be less complicated, now that she'd said she'd take any of his commands.

He narrowed his eyes. Somehow, he didn't believe her.

***

Kim rushed to her cabin and flopped on her bed. Her heart was still stammering, her limbs shaking. The rush of falling off the boat, seeing him jump in after her like some freaking super hero. Seeing how he moved in the water.

Seeing his chest, all wet and sexy like.

Damn. And then she'd kissed him. Had she said something about obeying his every command? Only in the bedroom maybe. She'd just been trying to think of a way to get closer, to put her lips over his perfect, seemingly-carved-out-of-granite ones.

And oh, what a kiss it had been.

And what a mistake.

Because when she kissed him, she knew for certain. This was her mate. And she wasn't allowed to have one. Her whole life, she'd been groomed to take over for her father as head of his law firm, hopefully after picking a suitable mate from the kids of one of his friends.

She didn't get to choose, and she didn't think he'd care about fated mates, if he even believed in them. But when her lips had touched Sebastien's, no, even before that, when he'd rescued her, she'd felt something so right. Felt the animal in her respond and say *this is your mate*.

Damn. Now it would be ten times harder to go back.

She'd just wanted a few more weeks of fun before settling down. Her father had picked a suitable candidate with bear blood, and though she hadn't met him, he was everything her family expected from her. She'd been wild growing up, and she'd been allowed, as long as in the end she met their rules.

So here, she just be wild, as she'd always been, a little longer. A hot fling with the ship's captain would have been fun. Now it was doomed to just end in heartbreak.

Now, when she walked away, it wouldn't be from a hot captain. It would be from her mate.

At least she thought he was. Why else would she have felt a swirl of cold from his animal, and known instantly that he was pure blooded polar bear? A large, fierce

41

predator. A perfect mate and protector for her young.

But it wasn't to be.

At least she understood her obsession with vexing the man and getting his attention. Sure, he was gorgeous, but it was more than that.

He was hers. Her wonderful, grumpy, fabulous long-haired pirate rescuer.

And now she needed to keep her distance. She went to change and then realized the others were out with their snorkels. Why should she miss out? She put on a short black swim skirt because her sarong had been lost when she went overboard, and tidied her braids in their ponytail, and then went back out as if nothing had happened.

As if she still didn't feel slightly shaky.

Maybe she should get something to eat. She walked into the small kitchen at the end of the bedrooms. It was curved due to the shape of the boat, and there were coolers set on the table full of various sundries. She picked two coolers up and headed upstairs.

She wanted to keep busy. If she stopped, she'd end up thinking, and that wouldn't be good. Not when all her thoughts revolved around what she wanted to do to her delicious mate.

She walked up on deck and people were seated here and there on deck chairs. She set the coolers down and pulled out a sandwich for herself, which she unwrapped and began to eat as she stared out at the ocean.

She wasn't sure what people found so magical about it. Yes, it was big. And blue. And wet. And it could kill you if you approached it wrong. And there were fish in it.

And it could be the most beautiful color, sort of like Sebastien's eyes. She looked up and saw him talking to the married couple. He was still soaking wet but was walking around like it was business as usual, like he had to jump off his boat to rescue wayward black women every day.

He was all calm and presence, and just being on ship with him made you feel more confident.

He seemed to feel her eyes on him because he slowly

turned and met her eyes with his. Damn, those blue irises seemed to sizzle into her. That wet hair that fell around his face begged to be teased back into place.

She was just the one to do it. She'd felt his response when she'd kissed him. He hadn't been against it. Would it really hurt that much more to leave after experiencing as much as she could with him for two weeks, rather than just staying distant and leaving after?

She didn't think so. On top of that, she didn't think she could stay away if she tried.

"Captain," she called out, gaining his attention again. He raised to full height, as he tended to do when he faced her, as if he wanted to remind her he was bigger, and taller, and in charge.

"Yes?"

"Will you be snorkeling with us today? I'm not sure we should be out there on our own," she said, one corner of her lips pulling up in a playful smirk.

He frowned. "Bart is captain on this trip."

She pursed her lips. She kept forgetting because it just seemed like wherever he was, he should be in charge. It looked like he felt the same. He looked put out by having to correct her about his title. "What should we call you then?"

"Mate," he said, flashing white teeth. "As in first mate. Or Sebastien."

She gulped and tossed her hair back. It was a habit, one that made her feel powerful. Sebastien it was then. She wasn't about to go calling him mate and reinforcing in her stupid brain that she should somehow think of him that way. Things would be bad enough as it was.

"Sebastien, will you be snorkeling with us today?" she asked, tossing her braids over her shoulder against the wind that insisted on tossing them forward.

He looked her up and down again and she stood firm and tall. Maybe he was trying to make sure she was really okay after falling off the back of the boat. Maybe he was just checking her out, which made her body heat head to toe.

But maybe something else went on behind those caribbean blue eyes. There was really no way to know. Not unless he told her, which he didn't look likely to do anytime soon, based on the clenched state of his jaw and the slight purse to those sculpted lips.

Oh well. They didn't need to talk about their feelings. He just needed to get in the water with them so she could snorkel behind him and hopefully look up his swimsuit.

Ha ha. Just kidding. Probably.

"As captain I should stay with the ship," Bart said helpfully. "So I guess you'll need to supervise the guests on this one."

Sebastien turned to him with a glare at the betrayal, and she thought she saw a faint gleam of satisfaction in the smaller man's eyes. "Bart…"

"I'll need you to check the anchor, anyway," Bart said, reaching into a compartment under the seat and handing Sebastien a snorkel and mask.

Sebastien looked at them in distaste. "I like to be on the ocean. Not in it."

She laughed. "Okay pretty boy," she said, putting an arm around him and pulling him toward the back of the boat where the others were climbing down to the small deck on the back of the boat to get off. Several were in the water.

"Don't call me that," he muttered.

"But you are," she said.

He muttered something else under his breath, but she ignored him. He could be grumpy if he wanted, but she intended to enjoy the day.

Wilson was walking out below them and putting on his mask as he went.

When we saw them he gave an appreciative stare and a whistle, and Sebastien's sharp gaze whipped to him in an instant.

"Not appropriate," he said.

"Fine," Wilson said. "It wasn't for you anyway."

Sebastien took a long, slow breath, and Kim felt a slight sense of impending doom. Right before a long leg reached out, kicked Wilson right in the ass, and sent him flying into the ocean in front of them with a slightly girlish scream.

She stifled a laugh, waiting to make sure Wilson was okay when he came up, coughing. But he gave her a big grin and a thumbs up, seemingly unruffled.

"You aren't getting in with that idiot, are you?" Sebastien said, pulling her to the side. "We could just eat lunch."

"Are you kidding?" she said, putting on her mask. "This is the vacation of my life. No way I'm going to waste a second of it."

He tilted his head, like the concept of vacation was foreign to him. After all, this was his job, not his vacation, and he didn't seem like someone who relaxed very often.

But she had a feeling that he'd get in the water if she did. So she put on her fins and walked awkwardly to the edge, and jumped off in an awkward back roll.

The water was the perfect temperature, cool enough to be refreshing, warm enough that you didn't need a wetsuit to not get chilled. The water was such a beautiful color, it had to be the most beautiful water in the world.

She whipped back to look at Sebastien, who was still glaring at the snorkel and mask, which looked hilariously tiny next to him. It was easy to forget the sheer size of the man, due to his gorgeous hair and pretty boy face.

But he was tall, taller than any man she'd been interested in, and as he finally gave in and pulled his shirt off to reveal his bare chest, gleaming and tan, the muscles beneath were huge and rippling. Just one of those men who could naturally get huge when working out.

Her mouth literally watered. What she wouldn't do to have a man like that in her bed. Just once...

He turned to go back into the cabin, probably to change into his swimsuit, giving her a view of his wide, powerful back and shoulders, which tapered down to a trim waist and a perfect—

"Want to snorkel with me?" A deep, masculine voice interrupted her thoughts.

"What?" she flipped around to see Wilson in the

water. He normally would have caught more of her notice, but he just paled next to the chemistry she felt instantly with Sebastien.

But he certainly seemed more interested in her than the latter was.

"Want to pair up with me? The others are paired."

"Oh, sure," she said. "Where to?"

"How about just the other side of the boat? There's not a lot out here, just coral and fish, but it's nice to just go face down and cool off."

"Sure," she said reluctantly, eyeing the boat. She kind of wished she could go with Sebastien, but he was still changing. Plus, he'd made it clear he wasn't interested, and there was no reason to be cruel to Wilson.

She tightened her mask, put her snorkel in her mouth, and swam forward with her face in the water.

Immediately the underwater world opened up to her. Blue and shimmering and wonderful. She felt ripples from Wilson swimming alongside her, but didn't pay much attention. At one point he reached for her hand, maybe just to make sure they didn't pull apart, but she moved out of reach. She didn't want to give him the wrong idea. She'd had plenty of men come on to her in her day and knew that it was best to be firm about rejection.

She looked over at him in the water as he pulled his hand back but he didn't seem overly bothered.

After another minute, she felt him catch her hand again. This time she shook him off more intentionally and swam a bit faster ahead. This wasn't a love cruise, even if she did want it to be that way with the captain. She shouldn't have agreed to go with Wilson.

Then something grabbed her leg, and she got pissed. She kicked hard, felt a connection with something and surfaced, pulling off her mask and sputtering in rage. The nerve of some people—

She stopped with a gasp when she shook water out of her eyes and saw Sebastien, red-faced with a hand over his perfect nose, eyes angry as all hell and burning like blue flames under the caribbean sun.

"I assume you have a reason for assaulting someone who was just trying to warn you you were getting too far from the boat."

She whipped her head around to survey her surroundings. He was right, she was a little too far from the boat and definitely should have turned back to stay with the group. Wilson's snorkel was a little ways away. Clearly he'd taken her rebuff well and had given her some space.

Too much space.

There were currents out here and she could feel herself being pulled away from the boat. She started swimming back toward the boat, feeling grim embarrassment for having assaulted the captain thinking it was Wilson and thinking he was making a move.

Of course the captain would only touch her for completely honorable reasons.

She gritted her teeth and swam past him, too humiliated to make a response, but he caught her by the arm.

"Hold on, swim back with me. The currents here are bad."

She looked into his blue eyes, that gorgeous blond hair streaming around his face. His touch on her arm was too much. Her embarrassment melted into something else entirely. Something warm, hot, and pleasant in an anticipatory sort of way.

They'd done nothing but fight since they met, and yet she couldn't help feeling she'd rather spend time with him than anyone else in the word.

Given the appraising look he was giving her, despite all his protesting, it was possible he felt the same way.

He tried to link an arm though a strap of her lifejacket but she pushed him off.

"I can swim on my own," she said, setting out ahead of him.

"Fine, stubborn female," he said, striking out ahead of her.

They battled for first position, and soon they were

passing their group, reaching the ship, and panting and looking at each other as the others dove and splashed.

He pulled off his mask and put it on the swim platform. His face was tensed, lips pursed, but there was something glinting in his blue eyes. Something she hadn't seen before.

Pleasure.

"That was fun," he said, hefting himself up to sit on the low platform and reaching a hand down for her to do the same. "You know, I've never really gotten in with the customers before. It's nice."

"Shouldn't you try what you're selling?"

He shook his head, sending sparkling water droplets spraying around him. Damn he was beautiful. All that muscle, tanned and dripping wet. "What I'm selling is a safe voyage where everyone can enjoy themselves. Nothing more, nothing less."

"How do you know it's enjoyable if you never try it?" she asked.

He looked out at the ocean, and she noticed a familiar gleam in his eye as he did. He loved it. He surveyed the ocean the way she surveyed anything that looked fun or adventurous.

He was a man of singular passion. It was almost good that he was destined not to be with her. She wouldn't want to have to compete with the ocean. Especially for her mate. That would hurt.

Not as much as having to walk away from him and go back to New York to keep family promises that were made before her birth, but yeah, it would hurt.

"I'm glad you got me out here. I'm even glad my dad made me first mate instead of captain, though I was pissed at first. Maybe I did need to relax." He rubbed his nose and glared at her playfully. "Why did you pop me one though? Can't say that was enjoyable."

She tried not to laugh, because it wasn't funny, but looking back on it, the situation kind of was. "Sorry, I thought you were Wilson."

He expression darkened as he looked her over.

"What?"

Oh shit. Then she'd have to explain why she accidentally kicked Wilson, and she didn't even know how much Wilson had actually pulled. And he looked angry at her.

She should have just claimed she accidentally kicked too hard. She bit her lip.

CHAPTER 4

He didn't like the dark feelings stirring within him. Anger, possession, jealousy.

And the fear he'd experienced when he's seen her swimming past her snorkeling partner, getting too far from her boat and out toward dangerous ocean currents.

It was similar to how he'd felt when she'd flown off the back of the boat. Like his heart had stopped and only had permission to start again when she'd been okay.

He'd never felt this way before. He'd always been a protective sort of person. Always wanted to protect his family and the people under his care on the ship.

But this was different. A soul deep need that seemed to burn within him.

And he didn't know what to do about it.

And now he was feeling it again, as she said that she'd kicked him thinking he was Wilson. So what had Wilson done? He had his own suspicions about Wilson. He wasn't sure exactly what kind of shifter Wilson was, but he was something. And he'd been one of the last people to book the boat, after the couple.

So had he done it because Kim had booked it, and he could sense Kim was an alpha female, a rarity in the shifter world? It was something to watch out for.

He tried to convince himself it was because she was just a passenger, but he couldn't help feeling there was something else to it.

Her warm gray eyes sparkled in the afternoon sun. Her dark hair was dotted with glistening drops of water, and her curvaceous, tall body was graceful in the sea. She was some kind of sparkling water sprite, and he found himself wanting to watch out for her for the rest of his life.

Which was stupid, because she was a lawyer. She was going back to New York, back to "civilized" life. She didn't need him. She'd play and have fun like many of the tourists here, and then go back to the "real world".

Leaving everything behind.

Like his mom had left him and his brothers and his father behind. True, the location had been different, but the result had been the same. Sebastien had seen the destruction it wreaked on his dad's heart and he wasn't going to open himself to the same. Not to mention how damaging it had been for him and his brothers, suddenly rejected and on their own.

Their dad had tried to explain that they were part animal, some more than others, and that animals didn't usually stay together in the wild. Especially bears like them.

So after their mom had left, making excuses about it being too cold, their father had moved them to the tropics. Polar bears didn't need to live in the Arctic. In fact, their bodies had to go through intense changes to do so, storing tons of fat to stay warm.

Here in the tropics, as long as there was water, they were fine.

But he couldn't help thinking that part of the reason his father had come here was in the hope that his mother would show up one day.

But she hadn't.

He heard Kim clear her throat and made an effort to pull out of his thoughts and be less rude. What had they been talking about? He looked to her for a clue and she gave him an innocent look as jealousy coiled through him again.

Wilson.

"What did he do?" he growled, a little more harshly than he meant to.

She bit her lip and looked to the side. Her lashes sparkled with water. So long. "Nothing."

He exhaled tensely. "Sure. No, what did he do? I'm captain, you have to tell me."

Her eyes twinkled and she swam a bit away from the platform. "Maybe I'll tell Bart later then."

He slid into the water to chase her. The others were on the other side of the boat so they didn't see her make a break, giggling, to evade questioning.

But she was smaller than him, something his body kept noting even as it noted that she was also strong and vivacious, and it was easy to catch up in a couple of strokes. Within minutes he had her against his body, and once again, he liked the feeling far too much.

She struggled helplessly and then gave up against him, looking up into his eyes with ones that gleamed like polished silver in the sun. "Fine, I give," she said, biting her lip and pushing her long braids over her shoulder as she looked up at him.

"Good," he said, still encircling her in his arms, telling himself it was so that the current couldn't pull her away. "Now tell me what happened with Wilson."

"He made a move on me," she said. When he let out a low growl, she corrected herself. "Just tried to grab my hand a couple of times. I don't know, I didn't look back after the first one, maybe that was you."

He tried to keep the anger down in himself. He didn't like the violent reaction he had to another man coming onto her. It suggested things about his bear that he didn't like. Like that he had found his mate. And he was never going to let something like that dictate his life the way it had his father's.

But the Wilson thing, that was worrying. Should he tell her outright about the shifter thing? Presumably she already knew that he could sense her and she could sense him. But had she picked up on Wilson yet? The man wasn't a very strong alpha and wasn't putting out a very intense scent.

"You should be careful around him," he settled for saying. "Maybe not go off alone with him."

She nodded. "Yeah, I think I'm in agreement there," she said. Then she gave him a playful look that made him want to take her close and kiss her. "But who will be my partner?" She gave him a coquettish stare.

Damn, she made it hard to stay serious. Or angry. "Me," he said. "I'll partner you."

He only meant it for activities, but it seemed to mean more once the words hit the air, taking on a flavor that was slightly romantic. "It's only for a few days," he amended. "Not a big deal. I'm enjoying being out in the water anyway," he said.

She went silent then, as if considering everything he'd said, everything that had passed between them. Maybe this female was more serious than he'd first thought. She'd seemed so flippant, whether she was stealing his boat or making fun of him for losing his captain position, or falling off the back of the boat.

But she was a lawyer. There was a smart brain inside that tenacious body. She pushed out of his arms and broke the magical contact between them, becoming that irritating female that was always in trouble once again. She swam away with a laugh.

"We'll see. Maybe you and Wilson can take turns," she said.

"Not if he makes a habit of touching you when you haven't asked for it," he said with a growl.

She turned back with a grin, a few feet away in the water. "He's not the only one."

That was it. He swum after her and caught her again, taking her by the arm and whipping her back against him so he could take her lips in a hard kiss. She gasped in shock but he smothered it with his kiss, diving deep, swiping possessively through her with his tongue, owning and claiming and letting her know he was a man who took things seriously, even if it was kissing some sense into the most beautiful, frustrating, infuriating woman he'd ever met.

When they pulled away, she was gasping. There was fury in her eyes, along with something else. Something much more primal that called to him.

"Honey, you've been begging me for it from the moment you saw me," he said gruffly, keeping a hand around her soft waist. "And if you pretend it's the same with anyone else, I'm going to give it to you."

She bit her full lower lip and gave him half a grin, but then swam away once again, giving him no answer to his statement. He couldn't tell if she was overwhelmed, like he felt, or if she just had nothing to say.

But he had a feeling that he'd won this round, for the first time between them.

***

Kim watched as the others took plates to the barbecue and then sat to eat. She'd gotten her plate earlier, scarfed down what seemed like the appropriate amount of food, and been brooding and nursing a single wine cooler ever since.

The breeze was cooling, the sun was casting beautiful streams of orange and pink and yellow across the darkening red sky in front of her, and the water was turning dark blue and reflecting the sunset.

And she still hadn't forgotten that single kiss that had rocked her world.

Sebastien was nowhere to be seen while Bart was handling the grill. They were still anchored out here in the middle of this beautiful ocean, with nothing visible in the distance. Tonight she'd be sleeping in a tiny cabin, not to far from his, dreaming of pulling his hair out of that beautiful ponytail and winding her fingers in it as she took his lips in a kiss that was revenge for what he'd done to her in the water.

Not the kiss, but telling her that she'd been begging for it. It didn't matter that he was right. She checked her watch and waited for the others to finish eating. Wilson kept giving her smiling glances, pushing his thick blond hair out of his face in an attempt at flirting.

The couple was a little standoffish. She got the feeling that the wife found her threatening, which was a shame, because she could have used a girl friend on this voyage. She couldn't wait to get back and talk to Mara. She pulled her phone out of her tote bag and checked again for bars. Nothing.

She'd just have to wait until dark. She had a plan. One she was sure her handsome captain would object to, but she had already figured out a way around it.

She was pulled from her thoughts by Bart sitting next to her with a plate of his own. The smell of grilled chicken lifted toward her nostrils as he cut in and chewed, looking thoughtfully out at the ocean. Where else was there to look?

"Don't be too hard on the captain."

She chuckled. "He's not captain. You are."

He laughed, a sound like a small dog's bark, and slapped his knee. "You know as well as me that no matter who's piloting this vessel, he'll always be thought of as the captain."

She laughed and put an arm around the smaller man. He blushed and focused on his chicken. He looked to be around Sebastien's age, maybe a little older. But Sebastien commanded more attention and respect, and the other man didn't seem to resent it, even if he did seem to be aware of it.

"He hasn't had a lot of time for fun. His father wasn't trying to be cruel or anything, but you can't get the captain to enjoy himself. He's been trying to run things since he was little. Since I was little. If he ain't in control he don't know what to do with himself."

She smiled. "I guess I'm a good counter to that."

He grinned back. "That you are. Stealing his boat, falling off of it. Getting too far away while swimming. And other things." He smirked slightly and looked away, and she realized he must have seen them kissing. Of course, since he wasn't in the water, what else would he have been doing?

"No no, don't feel guilty," he said. "I guess all I'm saying is, whatever you're doing, keep doing it."

She smiled. That would be no problem. She even intended to start up again as soon as the sun was down. As soon as the others took to their cabins and were safely asleep. Then she'd enact her plans with the captain.

***

Sebastien was on his back, listening to the quiet sounds of the ship rocking at night, when a knock sounded at his door. He sat up a little too quickly and nearly whacked his head on the low ceiling of his cabin.

"Who's there?" he hissed.

"Shh…" a feminine voice answered, as the door to his cabin opened. He grimaced. He should have locked it, but he didn't think anyone would have dared to bother him.

But of course Kim never held to anyone's expectations. She was in the doorway, wearing another one of those sensuous bikinis that pressed up her breasts in the middle, in bright colors that complimented her smooth, dark skin and lush curves. And a low sarong about her wide hips. Her legs were long and toned, her stomach curved in like an hourglass, with soft fat on the front that he wanted to sink his hands into.

She was soft, womanly and perfect, and he longed to take her in his arms and show her.

But she wasn't for him, he reminded himself for the last time. She was a city girl, and he wasn't looking for a mate. He wasn't looking to be destroyed like his dad was.

Still, he found himself wondering what just one night with this gorgeous woman would be like. One night together with no strings attached.

Now that was a dangerous thought. He had a feeling that once he found a home inside that body, those arms, that he'd never be able to let go. And that thought scared him more than anything.

"Why are you here?" he asked, standing and shutting the door behind him.

"I'm trying something I've never done before and wanted to see if you'd join me."

"What do you mean?" he asked, eyes narrowed.

"I'm thinking of going skinny dipping."

He bit his tongue and then swore. "And you came to tell me this why?"

"I don't think it's safe to go alone."

He folded his arms, shifting his weight to try to ignore the erection growing in his pants as he thought about her curves, half covered by dark water, glistening in the moonlight. "Damn straight. It's not safe either way, because I'm not going. It would be unprofessional, not to mention unhygienic."

"Oh please," she said, taking a step forward to place a hand on his chest. He could feel his heartbeat hammering away beneath it and hoped she wasn't aware of it. But when she looked up with a grin on her face, he could tell she was. "Like anything about the ocean is hygienic." She played with the neck of his shirt, pulling it down slightly, teasing the hair of his chest. "It's wild, untamed, exciting. And natural. That's what people love about it."

That's what I love about you, he wanted to say. But it made no sense. All the woman did was frustrate him.

"But if you're not interested, I suppose I could go ask Wilson," she said, turning to leave.

"Like hell," he growled. When she turned to him with a satisfied smirk, he knew she'd gotten him. But damned if he'd let another man see her naked curves in the moonlight. He didn't know exactly what this was between them. Didn't know why she was the first woman he'd kissed in ten years. Didn't know why it drove him out of his mind to think of another shifter pursuing her.

And if he did know, he didn't want to acknowledge that.

All he knew was that she was his. Or she could be tonight. And if they didn't go all the way, at least he could see her naked.

Naked in the ocean with a woman as free as the wind. The idea appealed to him. "I'll change and be right out."

"Change?" she asked.

"I'll come out in my swimsuit. I'm not promising more," he said.

"Tit for tat," she said cryptically, winking at him before slipping out and shutting the door behind her. "I'll be waiting for you in the water."

No words had ever made him so hard.

CHAPTER 5

When he slipped out onto the lower back deck and stepped down onto the swim platform, she was already waiting in the water. He'd changed quickly so that she wouldn't have to wait, and because he worried about her out on the deck in the dark.

The others had exhausted themselves and retreated to their cabins, and he'd forbidden them from coming out in the dark before Bart knocked on their doors. They couldn't risk people getting hurt at night.

But he was a light sleeper and tended to stay awake on nights like this, making sure no one got any bright ideas about night swimming without waking the staff. And he'd just been lucky that she'd decided to come to him first after all. Not Wilson.

There would have been a pretty intense confrontation if he'd had to find them together, naked. He gritted his teeth and told himself it was just about propriety, but as he saw her emerge, kelpie like, from the water after dipping her head under, he knew it was much more than propriety he was worried about.

He was worried about his heart.

He sat on the platform in his board shorts and watched her tread water. "Are you…" How did one ask such a thing?

She shook her head and then dunked under water, leaving her braids floating above her. When she surfaced, she had a grin on her face and a piece of material in her hand, and she tossed to him. He caught it with a stern look at set in on the swim platform. He'd only held it for a second, but he knew the feel of a built-in bra when he felt one.

Warmth moved up into his neck and other uncomfortable parts of his body as he saw the tops of her beautiful, smooth breasts in the water. She was glistening, glorious, and he wanted nothing more than to get into the water and make her his. Like he was some cursed ship captain and she was some damn harpy or mermaid calling him to his doom.

She went under again and this time surfaced with the

sarong, which she handed him. His mouth went dry. That meant there was only…

She went under again and tossed him small swim bottoms. He gulped and adjusted his sitting position. Damn, not a stitch on. He longed for more light so he could see her beautiful body fully illuminated. He could only make out the vague shape of it, the curve of her, down to her dark legs that fluttered in the water. Her smooth shoulders glistened with ocean water, those gorgeous braids floated around her tantalizingly. He wanted to put his hand in them and pull her close for another possessive kiss.

She opened those full, perfect lips and her eyes glistened playfully in the moonlight. "Your turn," she said.

He swallowed. It was now or never. Be the stern ship captain he'd always been who'd never allowed himself fun, never gone out of line, never taken a risk, or get in the water with this magnificent creature who pulled him to do things he'd never considered, feel things he'd never imagined.

He was a straight person, and his path had always been in a line. She was a magnet pulling him off his track, but he couldn't help but like it, even as a part of him felt dimly that this was going to be his doom.

"Come on in," she said, grinning and moving the water around, causing her breasts to rise and fall in the water in a tantalizing way that made his mouth dry. "The water's fine."

The cool ocean breeze swirled around him as he slipped into the ocean, letting the cool water caress his skin as he swam toward her. With one smooth motion he reached down, undid the tie of his shorts and slid them off to toss them on the swim platform.

Her eyes heated and locked on his, then ran down the length of his body.

They were naked. This was stupid. He wasn't looking for anything but tonight, and she wasn't the type he was looking for if he was.

But still, he ran his hands over her smooth waist, put one hand in her braids to cradle her head, and pulled her to him, relishing in the smooth feel of her curves against him as he took her mouth for the second time.

Her body was warm and soft, plush against him as he made love to her with his mouth. He kissed her lips, her neck, her shoulders, all bared to him and salty in the ocean, but it didn't matter. He kicked to keep them treading water as he explored her body.

His hands dropped to her chest and he gently kneaded her smooth bared breasts. "You're so gorgeous. You infuriate me in every way, but you're gorgeous," he said.

She wrapped her arms around him and leaned back, offering herself up to him. "I'm not looking for anything serious."

"You won't get it from me," he growled, lowering to water level to lick at her nipple. She tasted salty but it felt just right. He arched her farther back and kissed her navel, dipping his tongue along the center. The more he touched her, the more he tasted, the wilder her body felt, the more the bear within him roared for his mate.

But he knew how stupid it would be to answer that call.

She had her life, he had his. It wouldn't do to pretend that being mates would solve all of that. But that didn't mean they couldn't experience all of this chemistry together.

She flailed slightly in the water and he pulled her closely, keeping them afloat. "When you're touching me, I can't seem to focus on not drowning."

His eyes grew serious as he made her a promise. "I would never let you drown. I would never let anything happen to you."

Her eyes widened, like his statement meant something to her, like no one had ever said that before. The thought of it made him angry. This beautiful woman should be protected. She was strong and fiery and beautiful and precious, and yet protection seemed to be wanting in her life.

He pulled her close and just held her. Was he really protecting her by taking what he wanted with no thought for the future?

She ran her hands over his shoulders. "I can't promise you more than tonight, but I really want tonight. Just one night with my captain."

He swallowed, still holding her, letting the cool water pass them, keeping each other warm with their bodies. What to do? The bear inside him ached to know his mate at least once, and it wouldn't do to ignore his bear. But the human in him resisted a match that made no sense. She was everything he wasn't. She'd be bored with him for sure, and he'd get angry with her.

So why wasn't he letting her go? Why was he dipping to kiss the shell of her ear? Why was he grasping her large, soft butt in his hands and wrapping her legs around his waist in the water so he could keep her afloat? What was wrong with his brain today?

Damn, his father was a good matchmaker. The problem was neither Sebastien nor Kim wanted to be matched. And at least it was fair. She didn't want commitment anymore than he did. The thought bothered him slightly, but at least it was fair. If she had wanted him for keeps, he could never condone doing what they were about to probably do.

But just one night, with only the ocean as witness, the sound of waves drowning their passion, alone, what could that hurt?

Maybe a lot, but he felt he'd hurt more if he didn't have it. After this he could go back to the sea and she could go back to New York, and they'd each have a pleasant memory to treasure.

He took her hand and swam toward the little dinghy he'd brought out with him when she'd stolen the boat. That seemed like an eternity ago, when she'd only been a nuisance. His dad had tried to describe to him just how quickly the mate thing happened, but he'd never believed it, always thought his dad frivolous and shallow. Not that he blamed his dad for what happened afterward, but he had to believe his dad had made some sort of mistake that could be avoided. Because otherwise how could he prevent the same thing happening to him?

He imagined building a life with this woman, enjoying

everything with her, having cubs with her, and having her be gone one day. The imagined pain of it struck him down to the bone.

That's why this just had to be a passionate night to lose oneself in. One where they both knew the rules and took whatever passion they could from one another while leaving their hearts intact. But a part of him wanted to know why she said she couldn't make promises. A part of him realized there was a part of her that was just as trapped as he was. And though he had no intention of getting out of his cage, he found himself wanting to free her if possible.

He climbed up into the boat and helped her up from the much smaller swim platform. The boat swayed. When she was safely inside and seated on the chair next to the captains chair, he untied the ropes holding them close to the other boat and let it out so they could drift away from the yacht.

The dinghy was a little large to be called a dinghy. It had only the two seats, plus a wide bottom and a motor on the back. They often towed it along on longer trips in case someone need to go for tools or gas or help or something.

He could still remember the feel of riding out here, chasing a wayward woman who had stolen his boat. How angry he'd had felt, but also, how excited. His life had been one thing for so long, and even thought it was uncomfortable to be different, he was sort of glad it was. And unsure how he would go back to normality after this.

He moved the cooler that made a makeshift bench onto the captains seat, reached under the bow to grab a few blankets they kept under there, and laid them on the bottom of the boat. There would be just enough room to hold her. They might not be able to do everything, but under the cover of darkness, they could do a whole lot.

He took her hand and helped her down onto the soft, makeshift bed he'd made. He wished he could give her something even greater. In the darkness, he could just make out the shape of her body, but he was reassured that no one from the boat would be able to see them at all.

He couldn't stand for anyone else to be able to see her. She splayed beneath him with a small smile and one arm over her head. Beautifully naked and reassured. He lowered himself down with her. It was so much easier to be stupid in the darkness.

***

Oh, she'd been wanting this for so long. She couldn't even say why or how. It wasn't just that he was a walking fantasy, that his hard body naked was more than she'd ever imagined. Here in the darkness it was quiet and private. There were clouds in the sky obscuring the stars and so she could barely make out the outline of his body. But still, she knew him. She reached up to feel along his sleek, damp, hugely muscled arms as he knelt over her. He was so tall, so powerful, and his hair whipped in the slight wind blowing at night.

She could make out faint light behind him from the boat, but it would just make them more invisible in the darkness to anyone who was used to the light.

No one would guess that they were out here in this little boat, about to make love like their lives depended on it. At least she thought so. Why else would he have taken care to give them privacy, to lay out clean towels for her comfort? Not that she cared about comfort again. All she really knew was that if he didn't touch her with those strong hands again or kiss her with that strong mouth, she was going to explode. She might explode either way.

He leaned forward, grabbing her other hand to pull it up with the one above her head. He pinned both hands there in one of his, and leaned forward to kiss her again. This time their naked bodies met, his thighs over hers, his chest rubbing her taut nipples. The sensation was nearly unbearable and she writhed against him.

He simply growled and pressed her hands back, as if to remind her who was in charge. Well, that was fine, but he couldn't expect her to simply lie there. She nipped his lower lip as he pulled back to come in for another kiss, and his hand tightened on hers. Not hurting her, but just letting her feel the strength of them.

Yes, my mate, her bear murmured.

But we aren't allowed to choose, she said back. So just one night.

One night is never enough, the bear answered, bringing her close to the surface. Kim could almost feel her teeth changing, but she resisted the shift. The closer to shifting she was, the more she realized this beautiful man on top of her was hers and hers alone, forever. And that was just too painful to think about.

He parted her lips and kissed her more deeply, as a hand slipped between her legs to play in her folds. He slipped a finger over her center and rubbed lightly, making her arch and moan even as his hands held her in place and his lips stifled her kisses.

In the darkness, everything felt more intense. She couldn't see, so the scent of him, like clean ocean wind, the feel of him, like steel covered in velvet, and the sensations in her body, like fireworks, were all intensified by a hundred degrees.

Each touch was exquisite. His finger moved in gentle circles as his tongue teased. She met his thrusts with hers, swiping her tongue around his in a hot meshing that brought them closer and closer together. Dangerously close, as his circling finger got more and more precise in building the pressure rising inside her. Her breath came faster. She struggled against his arms and the impending release, gasping against his mouth, fighting the urge to scream out in anticipation.

He pressed down gently, in a slow circle, and that was enough. She arched and let out a scream that was only half stifled by the harsh kiss he gave her right after. He released her hands so she could clasp them around him, and she dug her fingernails into his back as wave after wave of sweet release hit her.

Nothing had ever felt this way. Nothing made sense anymore. She moved against him, wanting more, and he gave it to her.

"I want to taste you," he said, reaching for something on the floor. "Can I?"

"Sure," she said breathlessly. "Taste all you want."

He tied her hands in one of the towels, a gentle but strong knot, and placed the end under the heavy captain's chair. She struggled against it but once again found herself naked and at his mercy, with her hands above her head.

The captain definitely liked being in control. Lucky for him, she liked him being in control as well. He seemed to sense that, and she could almost see the flash of a smile when he knelt between her legs and spread them in front of him. How she wanted to see him smile in the light. What would that even look like, a full smile from this stern, devastating man?

But right now he had other things in mind, and his hands kept a firm grasp on her soft thighs as he lowered his head to swipe right over her with his tongue. She arched back, eyes nearly watering in pleasure at how good it felt when he kissed right over her center. He sucked gently, running his tongue back and forth over the most sensitive part of her, and she fought the restraints, his hands, the towel, fruitlessly. She was unable to escape his mouth, his touch, the pleasure threatening to overwhelm her.

But not for a moment did she feel trapped. Instead she felt safe, anchored, so that she couldn't float away. It felt like no one had ever cared for her in that way, and it hurt her feelings.

But right now, she would just savor the feeling of being totally safe and totally pleasured, as his tongue played and explored. He wasn't simply tasting her, he was learning her, and she could tell by the way his movements changed as her breathing and heartbeat sped up and her legs clenched and fought the oncoming pleasure that he was a very effective student indeed.

It was coming, it was coming, it was coming as she looked at the faint stars above her and held her breath as all her muscles tightened in anticipation. Then he murmured something against her and the brush of his lips set it all off.

She bit her lip to keep from screaming and arched back with closed eyes as the orgasm hit. Once again, he freed her, quickly untying the towel and coming forward to wrap himself over her. He caught her lips in a kiss as her hands wrapped around his back to claw long trails into him to communicate how she was feeling. She tasted herself on him but it felt so right.

Nothing in the world could feel as right as this. How could it only last one night?

He held her as the orgasm abated, not making any move for more nor looking like he planned on it. Instead, he took a clean blanket, wrapped her in it, and held her in his lap as he rested against the side of the dinghy, which rocked gently in the waves.

His breath was hoarse and husky, she could feel her own heart pounding in time to his. His hand found her hair and played at the base of her neck as her body tried to slowly calm. She felt so warm and safe against him. She didn't want to go back to the ship, back to civilization, or back to New York. She just wanted to stay here with her mate.

CHAPTER 6

They were both quiet as Sebastien pulled the rope in until the dinghy was once again right next to the bigger boat. He helped Kim silently onto the back of the boat and got on behind her. They changed into their discarded clothes, which were cold from the night hair, and then Sebastien helped Kim climb the ladder to the top deck for some inexplicable reason.

But she felt guided by him, so she went.

When they were up top, the cool, humid night air whipping around them, Sebastien went silently to the front of the boat and stood with his hands in his pockets, waiting for Kim to join him.

"What does this mean?" she asked him, coming beside him, longing for the warmth of his body, the feel of his touch, but knowing he hadn't promised anything like that. That nothing more could probably happen between them. Neither of them had made promises, except to enjoy one night together.

But could anyone stick to that after seeing how amazing things could be together between them?

He shook his head and walked below deck. She wasn't sure if she should follow, but a moment later he reappeared with a large blanket, which he wrapped around her shoulders.

"That was amazing," she said, unable to stand the silence any longer. "How are we supposed to pretend it didn't even happen?"

He pressed his lips together but just kept looking out at the ocean, infuriating her.

"Please, say something," she said. "It's worse if you just keep silent."

He shifted slightly, took a breath, but then let it out. She sighed and turned to leave, unable to sit and wait any longer, when he caught her arm and pulled her back. He looked into her eyes, and saw permission in them to pull her close, so he did.

She loved the warmth that surrounded her, but her heart still felt slightly cold. Then he spoke.

"I know I have no right to ask this of you. I told you, I'm not looking to make promises. But yes, I don't know how to forget what happened tonight because nothing like that has ever happened to me before. I don't know how to pretend it didn't happen, because it has struck me to my core. And I don't know how to not do it again because every cell in my body seems to scream to repeat it." His arms tightened around her, making her feel small yet secure.

As a strong, tall, curvaceous woman, it wasn't a feeling she was used to. But she liked it. Even if she knew this had to end at some point, she liked it.

"I know it's not fair."

"Why aren't you looking for something?" she mumbled against him.

"I just, it's not for me. I like my life how it is." But the tightness in his voice suggested there was more to it. But she had no right to ask, so she didn't.

"What about you?" he asked. "You said you weren't looking for anything serious. I'm not used to that from women. They seem to want commitment, at least at first."

She snorted and pulled back to look at him, wondering how he wasn't cold in the night air. It was warm in the caribbean but the water was cool and in the night air one could feel quite chilled. "Not all women. Plus, sometimes we already have a commitment. Elsewhere."

He pulled back with a shock, leaving her cold. "What do you mean?" His eyes were icy and hard, not the distant look he'd had when she first met him, but with a primal anger in them from something she couldn't identify.

She studied him for a minute, and then realized the implication. "No, no. Nothing like that. I'm not cheating. It's just that… sometimes families have certain expectations. I have…well, after this trip I have duties. To my family, I mean." She shrugged. "It's fine."

He raised an eyebrow. His thick hair was starting to dry and little wisps were raising to whip in the wind. It gave him even more of stern, pirate-esque demeanor and appearance. "I suppose that's admirable, that you put your family first."

That stung slightly, given how much it had always hurt to have to put everything she wanted aside for the family, but she supposed he was right. Filial loyalty was something to be respected.

"What was that expression?" he asked, coming forward again. Everything between them seemed to be a dance. Back and forth, back and forth, don't get too close, that could hurt. Don't get too far away, that could hurt worse.

She tilted her head and felt the wind over her braids. What was there to say? Even if he saw very real pain and distress over her situation, what could be done? Her family was powerful. She had her expectations. She shrugged. "It was nothing. I just sort of wish we could be reckless. That we could just enjoy my time in the Caribbean together, making love, enjoying the sun. Letting go a bit." She lowered her head slightly. "This is my last chance to let go."

His face tightened inexplicably at that. "I see. I'll think about it."

Her heart sunk. She'd put it all out there, and he had to think about it? Damn. If he felt like she felt, wouldn't he have just said yes, and damn the consequences? But no, he was all about rules and routines and regulations. He did everything according to what made sense, and nothing about them made sense.

She tightened the blanket around her shoulders and turned to go downstairs. But he caught her by the arm and pulled her back against him, planting his mouth over hers in a possessive kiss.

She gasped and then sunk against him, her mouth melting over his in a harsh, painful soldering of souls. Whatever they were playing with was going to hurt them incredibly, but she was somehow happy that he couldn't walk away either.

"I'm sorry," he said hoarsely, pulling away. But the next moment, he was taking her mouth again, like he had to taste her. Like he couldn't be away. He licked along her lower lip, making her open, and then licked inside her, exploring gently and fervently every bit of her.

He pulled back and leaned down, resting his forehead against her. "Damn it. I have a job. I'm not the captain here, but I still have things to do. Tell you what. My days are mine. My nights are yours. It's a shameless thing to offer, but something tells me you feel like me. That anything is better than nothing."

"And at the end?" she asked, knowing the answer but wanting him to answer without telling him.

"We walk away, grateful for what we had, but neither regretting or blaming the other."

But you're my mate, she wanted to say. But there was no point. Mate or not, she had her own reasons they couldn't be together. He could ask her the same, and she'd be the one who said no. He was right. This was the only option. No quarter. No begging.

She kissed him as her answer. Their relationship could be as silent as the night, and she could still have other fun during the day. It was a compromise, but she'd have to accept it.

After she crept away from him and quietly back to her bed, it took her hours to fall asleep. She couldn't stop picturing what they'd done in the dinghy, and the pain she'd seen in his eyes when he told her what they couldn't have.

***

The next morning when Wilson knocked on Kim's door, she was totally unready to wake up. They were going to another site to snorkel, and then to stingray city, a place where tourists could swim with rays, and then they would be heading back to the hotel.

Not that sex in a dinghy hadn't been nice, but she sort of looked forward to see what Sebastien could do to her in a fancy suite, or on the beach for that matter. She grinned as she told Wilson to go ahead without her and rolled groggily out of bed to get changed.

She pulled on her swimsuit and went up on deck in search of delicious coffee to keep her awake. Instead, she was greeted by the delicious sight of Sebastien, wide back revealed as the wind whipped his thin white shirt in the wind. As usual, he was at the helm and seemed completely at home there. Bart was over by the small counter where they had set up breakfast. He gave her an apologetic look and nodded toward Sebastien. She was guessing mere orders couldn't keep him from taking control.

She wanted to go over to Sebastien, ask about the day, talk to him. Just be near to him. But he'd said that his days were his, and his nights were hers, and that worked well enough for her that she hated to mess it up at all.

So she resisted the urge to go over there and went to sit by Wilson instead. He was wearing a hot pink shirt with a surfer logo on it. He seemed younger than her, in his mid twenties, though it could just be his demeanor. His blond, shaggy hair gave him a boyish look.

"What's wrong?" he asked, eyeing her suspiciously. "You seem super tired."

I was being ravished by the captain all night. No, that wouldn't work. "I didn't sleep well."

"Not used to being aboard a boat?" he asked, shoveling scrambled eggs into his mouth.

"No," she said. "Don't get a lot of chance to in New York."

"I didn't know that's where you were from," he said. "Tell me about it."

But even though she was usually friendly and open to talking about herself, she felt just a little too emotionally drawn to deal. "I'm not really in the mood. Tell me about you instead." Then she could tune in or listen as she wanted to.

"I'm from New York as well. My family is fairly prominent there."

"Oh?" she asked. "What do they do?"

He shook his head. "Naw, don't make me talk business."

She rolled her eyes and took a sip of coffee from a cup Bart handed her. Wilson had been the one to bring up his family but then didn't want to answer questions about them? Her eyes strayed to the handsome captain, then darted back to stare at the ocean beyond the boat.

Her whole body seemed focused on the next time she could be with her mate. Her bear seemed to be growling beneath the surface. She didn't know what to do to act normally, so she tried to talk to Wilson once again.

"So, what do you like to do?" she asked. "What brings you to the Caribbean?"

Wilson grinned. "That's two questions, what do you want me to answer first?"

She felt her patience snap. He was just being friendly and polite. Why did she seem to irritate her so much? She took a deep breath and reminded herself she was probably just letting her own stress and confusion rub off on Wilson. "Why are you here?" she asked, more bluntly than she meant to.

He didn't notice, simply put his plate down and stretched with a satisfied groan. When he relaxed back into his chair, he gave her a bright grin. "Just graduated school. Wanted to have some fun before settling down to more serious things."

Well, that she could understand. He was more like her than she would have thought. But that was why Sebastien intrigued her more than Wilson. He was the opposite of her, but that was interesting. Fully intent on duty, and yet his reason for not being with her was his own reason and preference, whereas for her, it was out of her hands.

In the end, the real one bound by duty was her.

***

Kim enjoyed the sting ray swim with that little tingle of anticipation that comes from having someone around that you are unbearably attracted to and who is unbearably attracted to you.

Sebastien stayed up on deck while they were down, but she couldn't help thinking of him, even as she fed the smooth, graceful gray creatures swimming around them. They liked to swim overhead and bump her or come around the front and move their soft bellies over her hands.

Most were snorkeling but Kim was diving, which allowed her to stay on the sandy bottom 12 feet beneath the others. She'd insisted on getting her scuba dive certification before the trip and now was sure it was worth it.

The Caribbean water was so beautiful and blue and clear, and she felt so weightless here, almost as if she could be one of the animals gracefully swirling around her.

She let out a long breath into her reg and the animals swam over the bubbles, as if they liked the ticklish feeling of them.

She wished Sebastien could be down in the water with her, but as usual, he was up taking care of his "duties". She supposed that was something she was coming to respect about him, but she also wished he was near at all times.

That was normal. He was her mate, after all. She wondered how long it would take for the ache to go away once she went back to New York. A part of her said not to go. But she knew that they were only half animals. They had their human side to listen to as well. They had to live in the human world much of the time, with logic and reasoning and careful marriages to those who were a good match based on social standing and location.

And then there was the shifter side that meant duty to family in extending the bloodlines. That would be solved too by her marriage. Her suitor was already chosen, in fact. Her father had offered to show her a picture, but she'd said no. She hadn't wanted anything to interfere with her last vacation before she was a married woman.

She knew it was sort of old fashioned, the way her family expected her to just agree to an arranged marriage. But Bears were dying out. Powerful clans had decided that perhaps the best way to deal with this was to pair suitable alpha females and alpha males. The wolf shifters had been doing this for some time to deal with a scarcity of alpha females, and they seemed to be having some success.

Bears weren't as social or organized as wolves due to scarcity of resources in their wild forms, but they were coming along. As were other, more rare species of shifters.

She held out fish from between straight extended fingers, so that the sting rays could glide easily over her hand and take the fish. It tickled and she giggled into her reg, expelling a long stream of bubbles. She almost turned to share the moment with anyone around her, since half the fun of anything for Kim was sharing it with another person.

But the others weren't with her, and the dive master leading the tour at this location was up near the surface, helping the snorkelers.

That was fine. She'd just enjoy the peace under water, and fantasies of Sebastien.

In only a few more hours, they'd be back on land, and then he'd have to keep his promise and give her what she wanted.

***

Sebastien resisted the urge to strap on a diving tank and go check on Kim. Even though every fiber of his being seemed bent on checking on her or being close to her, he knew he had to restrain himself. They weren't a couple who could just fall into a mating. They both had complications and needed to be careful in exploring what lay between them.

So he focused on packing things up and getting ready so that when they did dock, it wouldn't be too long before he could go to Kim's room and rock her world. He wondered how many times he'd be able to do that before he said goodbye to her.

His heart thudded at the thought, like a sea bed with an anchor dropped heavily on it.

When the swim was over, and all of the other swimmers were getting onto the boat and taking off their gear, he felt his heart speed up in anticipation. He'd never felt sexual anticipation like this.

When she finally climbed up the back ladder and stood in

the sun in a gorgeous blue bikini, hair sparkling as she shook it, dark skin glowing from the relaxation, smile flashing at him, curves working as she took steps toward him, he felt his body freeze completely.

The urge to take her, to claim her and make her his own, was nearly unbearable. He almost forgave his father for getting carried away and making a poor choice that devastated all of them.

The mating urge was nothing to mess with.

She took a towel from Bart with a polite smile and wrapped it around her waist as she approached Sebastien, wide curvaceous hips swaying slightly, her beautiful, ample breasts pushed up in the middle to glow in the sun.

His mouth watered. Was this beautiful woman really to be his? Even temporarily?

Then she opened her mouth and proved there was more to this woman than her stunning looks. She also had a knack for irritating him.

"Ahoy Captain!" she called out. She sat on a bench next to the captain's chair. The wind whipped around them and she folded one leg sexily over the other. Sebastien tried to keep his eyes focused out ahead, though they weren't driving anywhere yet. Not until the guests were dressed and safe.

She leaned in with a wicked gleam in her eye that said she'd been anticipating what would happen when they got to shore as much as he had. "So, Captain, you gonna let me hoist your mainsail later?"

His eyes widened as he stared at her blankly. Hoist the what? There was no mainsail on the....oh. He narrowed his eyes at her, sure he hadn't had the last of her teasing.

She looked around them and then put a hand out to touch his leg as she looked up at him with a grin. "You know, plunder my booty? I'll show you my chest. My treasure chest, that is," she said.

He sighed in frustration, both because she was being ridiculous and because he was getting achingly turned on and couldn't do anything about it.

"I'm not a pirate," he muttered huskily.

"Still, you can plunder my booty any day," she said with a laugh.

"I'll keep it in mind," he said with grated teeth. She definitely had a booty that any man would want to plunder. The thought made him instantly angry, and he gritted his teeth again at the thought, wanting to lock her away where no one could see her and he could pleasure her all day long. Then again, she'd never agree to that.

She misinterpreted his angry expression, apparently thinking her teasing was getting to him and so she should continue it. He stifled a grin and readied himself for the next awful joke.

"I know you want to dock in my harbor," she said. "It's nice and wet."

He couldn't help it. His mouth fell open. "Kim!"

Her grin widened and she shifted position slightly, flipping her hair over her shoulder to give him a better view of her magnificent breasts. Treasure chest indeed.

He swore at himself for buying in to her ridiculousness. When they got back to shore he'd show her for making him look ridiculous. He'd make love to her until she couldn't think of ludicrous puns or pirate idioms.

And he'd do it until she couldn't walk anymore.

She seemed to guess the direction of his thoughts from the intent look in his eyes and her full lips opened slightly as she ran her tongue slowly along them. Damn, he was hard nearly instantly. Everything she did tested his control, and he was a man very much used to being in control.

"Go downstairs and change. Then find somewhere safe to sit. It's going to be a bumpy ride and I can't have you falling overboard again."

"Isn't it safest next to you, then?" she asked, stretching dangerously and showing off her breasts and her soft waist once again. "After all, you're the one who knows the ship and the route best."

He had to agree that was sound. But she was driving him out of his mind with her sexual innuendos and silly pirate metaphors. "Fine, you can stay, if you stop the silly pirate stuff. I'm not a pirate."

She folded her arms and huffed as she looked out over the rail at the water passing by them. "Fine. But I wish you were. Pirates are hot."

He let out an exasperated groan. "I'm not even going to try to explain why that's not true."

"Fine. I'll shut up for now, but stay here. That way, you know the bumpy parts and can tell me when to hold on."

He'd tell her when to hold on, all right. When he had her

blindfolded and bound to his bed frame, screaming her pleasure as he drove her to pleasurable oblivion.

Yeah, he'd plunder all right.

CHAPTER 7

Kim didn't realize how tired she was feeling until she walked into her empty suite. Sebastien had said he had some things to take care of before he could come join her, and she should go take a nap.

Hopefully because he intended to tire her out all over again. Her mouth watered and her legs clenched at the prospect of her hot pirate taking control all over again. She grabbed two sheets of paper off the counter and took them to a hammock on her deck that overlooked the ocean.

The air was sweet and clean with a hint of something icy and cool, and she rocked slightly with one foot as she read over Leah and Mara's schedules to see if either one of them would be home today.

The last thing she wanted was to be caught having hot hammock sex with Sebastien when one of them walked in the room.

Then again, maybe he would take her to his room, wherever that was. She'd known that his dad owned the hotel, from when she'd met his dad the first day here, and if he did have a suite, it had to be pretty nice.

The one they were in was unbelievable, with tropical colors all over the cushions on the furniture and in beautiful paintings on the walls. The hardwood floor felt smooth and comforting after a long day on sand, and the views couldn't be beat. There were three bedrooms, one for each of the women, and they were all equipped with master baths.

She hadn't been anywhere like this since she'd graduated law school and started working 60 hour weeks at her father's firm. She'd managed to take breaks here and there for adventures, but it wasn't common. Her father understood her lust for adventure and had agreed to one last vacation, wherever she wanted to go. So here she was.

The problem was, she'd discovered a lust even greater than her need for adventure.

It looked like both Leah and Mara would be out until night. That meant awesome evening sex, hopefully. She kind of missed the chance to talk to the other girls. She was the type that liked to talk things over and it always helped her figure out her feelings, which she'd never been very in touch with.

She was very clear on her feelings for Sebastien, which made this all the harder. Not every shifter even had a fated mate, it seemed, so it was pretty unfair that someone like her should have hers, and yet not have it be the one she was destined to be with.

She was a woman in her thirties, she should be able to decide. She set the schedules aside and let out a deep sigh as she folded her arms and relaxed into the hammock.

She had been out late last night with Sebastien, and had slept fitfully afterward. Surely a little nap wouldn't be out of place. And then she'd have more energy for him to ravish her.

She thought of Sebastien in full pirate regalia, standing with folded arms and spread legs on the deck of a huge ship, with herself clasping his arm in a ridiculous dress like those on the covers of the bodice ripper romance novels she'd read in her twenties.

Oh yeah, that was that stuff, she thought as she drifted off to sleep. She was still muttering naughty things about pirates when Sebastien woke her several hours later.

***

She almost thought she was still dreaming. When she looked up into his intense, angelic face with the golden halo of his hair streaming around it, and saw that intense, concerned expression he wore. But when she reached up and felt his firm chest and heard the quick exhale of his breath, she realized no, he was real. All flesh and blood, all hers. She ran her hands lower, over his abs, and then noted his frown.

She looked out where he was looking, at the setting sun behind them. "It's getting late," she said. "I didn't mean to sleep so long."

"I know," he said. "Judging by the schedules on the floor next to you, your roommates will be getting back soon. Should we reschedule?"

She shook her head. "Hell no! I was promised this all day! Why can't we go to your room?"

He thought about it with narrowed eyes. She loved how

the icy blue-green color intensified when he did that. "I suppose. I haven't taken a woman there."

She put a hand up to stroke his hair. It was surprisingly coarse, but she supposed that happened when you spent a lot of time in the sun and the wind. "You don't allow yourself to have a lot of fun, do you?"

"I'm conscientious of how my actions impact others," he said, and she didn't miss the gentle censure in his voice. "I've always had responsibilities."

"Yes well, your dad doesn't seem to agree with your philosophy, does he? Why would he have set up all this matchmaking?" she asked.

Sebastien shook his head with a dark expression on his beautiful face. "My father and I disagree on many things. Some of them crucial." He reached for her braids. "Can I?" he asked.

"Asking permission isn't sexy," she muttered.

"No," he agreed. "But it's right."

"I wanted you from the moment I saw you," she said, watching him roll one of her braids between his fingers gently. Just having him close was heating her body.

"I know," he said, giving her a slight grin to let her know

he was teasing.

She swatted him and pulled her hair back from his grasp. He pouted and caught another braid, slowly winding it around his finger, pulling her gently closer. She pursed her lips as she came close enough to feel his hot breath. How many times had she kissed him at this point? Too many. Not nearly enough. She didn't know. All she knew was that as his lips lowered over hers, they made the perfect fit together, like two sides of a puzzle coming together.

She moaned softly and opened to meet his tongue, swirling against it with hers.

He groaned in response and wound his hand around her waist, holding her close, digging slightly into her softness. She knew she was a curvy woman, not some model, but she'd never felt anything but beautiful. And now, in Sebastien's arms, she felt something even more important than beautiful.

She felt treasured.

He continued the warm, soft but intense kiss and she felt something coiling inside her. So hot. So good it was nearly painful. Would she have to go without this for the rest of her life? She couldn't imagine. She couldn't even imagine not having him right now, so she pulled back to run a finger over his soft, gently curved lips. So perfect and velvety under her touch, as she was sure his member would be.

"So, which is it, pirate?" she asked. She pressed her finger against his lips in a shushing motion when she saw he meant to correct her. "Are we going to have to reschedule for tomorrow, or are you going to take me to your place? That is, unless you want to have spectators. I've never thought I'd particularly enjoy people watching, but if it's my only option at this moment, I don't think I could say no."

"Hell no," he growled, sounding nearly feral. "Hell no would I let anyone watch."

"Embarrassed by your technique?" she teased, as he slipped his hands under her legs and caught her easily up in his arms to walk toward the door.

"Hell no," he said, carrying her down the hall toward the elevator. "I'm just not going to let anyone but me see your body. Even if they are women." She laughed as they entered the elevator with an older couple who gaped openly at them.

Sebastien gave them an icy look. "What are you looking at?"

She almost felt bad for the couple, as they gave her a snobbish look and scuttled away. But she honestly couldn't summon up the strength to do so, not when she had so much to look forward to with the man of her dreams.

She held on to him as the elevator rose, treasuring this moment where she felt light as air and like everything in the world was right and wonderful. It wouldn't last forever, but it would last a little while.

That had to be better than nothing.

***

She was curvaceous and strong and tall, this beautiful woman in his arms. Yet she somehow seemed to weigh nothing as he walked into his suite.

He waited for her reaction to his obvious nautical obsession. From old nautical paintings he'd bid on on Ebay to the small ships in a bottle he'd assembled, to the spartan decorations around the huge suite, he wasn't sure how she'd take it.

But he needn't have wondered. She grinned and tapped his shoulder for him to let her down and then wandered around the apartment, looking here and there and touching this and that. She walked into his bedroom and he held his breath while he waited for her to come out.

When she did, she tilted her had and gave him an appraising look. He waited for her judgment.

She grinned. "It's so you."

He smiled. That was the perfect comment. She seemed to get who he was and be perfectly fine with that. She might be the first person in his life to do so. Everyone else would tell him to calm down, to be less restless, to stop doing everything at work and nothing outside of it, and to think of something other than the ocean.

But she simply understood what it meant to him, and it made him love her. It somehow made sense that he had made love to her for the first time on the ocean, rocking in a boat together. But what did she love?

She walked out to look at the view. It wasn't fancy. The suite was very high up, so that the beach and the people on it were blurry and small. But the view of the ocean? Unbeatable, rippling in blues and greens out into eternity, or at least until it met the silvery line of the horizon.

He joined her and leaned on the railing. The wind brought her scent to him and breathed it deeply, knowing it was going to be one of the things he missed most about her when she was gone.

She looked at him and the sunset reflected in her gray eyes. He could see himself in them, reflected just as he was, and it made him want to be a better man. A better person. And worthy of her.

But these were silly thoughts. They were just two people who would give in to their animal urges for a week and then go back to being the rational beings they were.

They had nothing in common. They didn't make any sense together. But somehow he still wanted to know everything about her.

He brushed her hair back and pressed a kiss to the base of her ear, where it met her jaw, and she shuddered against him. "What do you love, Kim?"

"What do you mean?" she said huskily, as he continued to kiss along the shell of her ear. She gasped as he ran his tongue along the inside of it.

"I mean, you know what I love. The ocean. What do you love?"

She frowned for a moment, as if she'd never considered it.

Then she sighed as his fingers played at the nape of her neck, tickling her lightly. "I guess adventure," she gasped out. He stopped teasing so she could finish what she meant to say. He wanted to hear all of it.

"I guess I always want to have adventures. I never want that to stop."

"Even when you're mated?" he asked.

"Especially then," she said. "I guess I'll just have to hope the man I marry has a sense of adventure. He'll be a bear, so that will probably work for him."

"You're a bear too, correct?" he asked.

She nodded. "Brown. You?"

"Polar," he said. "Probably some Kodiak in there too. We don't know that much about my mother's side of things."

A normal person might have left it there, assuming there was something painful about his mother that he didn't want to talk about, but not Kim.

"Why not?" she asked. "What happened? I mean, you don't have to tell me, but I'd feel dumb if I didn't ask."

"Kind of rude," he said.

"Maybe," she said. "But I'd rather seem rude than disinterested."

He raised an eyebrow at her. "As if anyone could ever think you disinterested," he teased in a low voice.

She grinned and he found himself loving that smile. It was lighting his world up, like a sunrise on the ocean, and he wanted to keep it around forever.

He kissed down her neck to her back and then along her shoulders, moving her hair as he went, enjoying the ocean wind and her scent and her soft sighs as he took his time touching her. There would be time for rough lovemaking later. Right now he just wanted to savor the moment and watch the sunset with her.

"Sebastien?" she asked, her voice hoarse.

"Yes?" he asked.

"If you don't take me into that bedroom and make good on your promises right freaking now, I'm going to burst."

He chuckled and continued his teasing, torturous kisses. "Just so you know, I hope you have many adventures." He stood and wrapped his arms around her from behind, pulling her back against his chest, holding her tight. "If the man you marry doesn't give you adventures, make sure to write and let me know."

He knew it was an absurd thing to offer. Why should she care to let him know? But he found himself needing her to say she would. He needed to know she was okay. She was his mate after all. Even if he didn't believe that mates were all they were cracked up to be, he'd felt too much for her too soon to be able to write it off completely.

No, he would always worry about her some, even if he knew that they couldn't possibly go together. She was a New York lawyer with a family expectation for who she would marry and he was a sea captain who had no responsibility for anything but his job.

It'd be a horrible match. But when she leaned up and whispered in his ear for him to take her, he found himself not giving a damn. He picked her up and carried her to the bedroom.

She giggled in pleasure. At least in this one way, they seemed to be perfectly matched.

CHAPTER 8

When he laid her on his bed, all he could think was that she looked perfect there against his sky blue sheets. A goddess with beautiful braids and a curvaceous, strong body that he wanted, no, needed to run his hands over completely.

He whipped her bikini off and tossed it beside the bed. Her breasts were even more beautiful in the light of his room than they were in the darkness on the dinghy when he could barely see them. So beautiful, perfect and round with dark nipples that begged for his attention. He immediately acquiesced, loving one and then the other with his mouth as she cried out in pleasure and arched, giving him even better access. He used his strong hands to gather the mounds together and licked a line along the inner curve where they met, and she cursed and then grinned at him to let him know it had been the good kind of cursing.

He continued to lick and play as one hand dipped to play with the waistband of her bikini band. He loved the feel of her soft curves all around it, her full, voluptuous thighs and wide, curvaceous hips. She was generously built and he could barely wait to be inside her. But he also wanted to savor every minute of their time together.

"I can't wait," she said. "I'm already wet for you." She reached for his hand and drew him over her. He looked into her sparkling gray eyes as heat surged through him. She was wet all right, and ready. The feel of her was heaven.

He ran his hands lightly over her breasts again, loving the silky softness of them, the heft of them in his hands. "You're so damn beautiful," he said.

She arched in response, loving his touch. He leaned forward to kiss each breast, licking and swirling his tongue until each nub was hard and aching and wet. Then he took each between his thumb and forefinger and pinched lightly. She gasped with a little scream and rolled sideways. He reached in the top drawer of his bedside table for a silvery tie. He grinned at her as he held it out in offering. He didn't mean to bind her for his own enjoyment, though he knew he'd enjoy seeing her writhe beneath him. No, he meant to bind her so that she could get more enjoyment than even her sensitive body would allow.

He wanted to make her feel so good that she felt she would explode, and then make it so she couldn't run away.

He looped the tie over one wrist and tied it in an intricate knot before tying it to his elaborately carved headboard. Then he took another tie and repeated it on the other side. Her breasts shook as she looked from side to side, then gave him a sly grin and parted her legs for him. Damn, he should tie those as well, but he didn't have time for that.

He stood and went to the bathroom to grab a condom. He carefully unwrapped it as he walked back into the center of the room to stare at his captive princess on the bed. He undid his pants and enjoyed the widening of her eyes and the way she bit her lip as his member sprang free. He was large, but he'd try not to hurt her. Hopefully she was experienced. He liked a woman who knew what she was doing.

He slid his pants all the way off and pulled his shirt over his head. All the time she stared at him like she wanted to eat him. Well, the feeling was mutual. His heart was threatening to beat out of his chest, he was more painfully hard than he'd ever been before, and an aching realization of just what she meant to him was starting to settle uncomfortably in his chest.

He knelt between her splayed legs and gently removed her bikini bottom. It was pretty, but what was beneath it was much prettier. He parted the lips gently and ran a finger along her, exploring and playing before dipping inside to test her.

He swore. She was so tight. He dipped another finger, then a third, stretching and stroking as she writhed and muttered expletives at him for taking so long. But one look at her heated, panting face told him she was enjoying it.

And he had to know that she was ready. Every impulse in his body made it impossible to hurt her. To the contrary, all he wanted to do was protect her, make her happy, make sure no harm ever came to her. And he needed it like he needed his next breath.

He'd never known anything like it before, and suddenly he needed to forget the strange sensation. So he put his hands on each of her soft knees, parted her legs, and then drove into her with one smooth motion.

It was a mistake. Being inside her didn't make him forget the uncomfortable feelings of love welling inside him. It intensified them by a hundred degrees. He settled over her, one hand on either side of her face. She looked up at him in wonder. Was she feeling these confusing things too? It was just supposed to be sex. It wasn't supposed to be so...*cosmic*. Right now, inside of her, he felt like they were part of something greater than them, and it was an incredible feeling, one he wanted more of and to escape from all at the same time.

She was his mate. He knew it more than ever. And he wanted to please her, so he began to move inside her. She uttered his name and wrapped her hands around his forearms as he pulled almost all the way out and then drove inside her.

Her tight velvet walls encompassed him, homing him and grounding him, and her little gasps of pleasure each time he moved drove him wild. Her body was quaking beneath him, beautiful breasts quivering each time he drove inside. Legs moving to encircle him. Tension building within him at an incredible pace. All he could see was her face, so beautiful, whether she was laughing in the sun or biting her lip and rolling her eyes back in anticipation of hopefully the best orgasm of her life.

He could tell the tension was building, as she reached up and put a hand in her hair and dragged slowly through her braids, pulling slightly. She murmured for him to hurry, then told him to slow down, then said to hurry again. Her glazed silver eyes seemed just as lost as he felt.

He reached between them to stimulate her externally as well as internally, because he felt like he was close to losing control inside. Her long-lashed eyes blinked up at him in amazement and her lips parted in a silent gasp that seemed to go on and on as her head flew back.

She was coming, gasping as she clenched around him, her velvet walls threatening to milk him clean before he was done pleasuring her. But he bit down and silenced the beast inside him. He would give her more orgasms, pleasure her so thoroughly that she couldn't walk right, even if it killed her.

He wanted her to remember him with every step she took.

***

The sensations rumbling through her seemed to go on and on, tearing at her very being, making her feel so very in love and so very heart broken at the same time.

She'd had sex but it'd never felt like this. She knew more than ever that he was her mate, and they were definitely playing with fire. Stars kept exploding behind her eyes like fireworks as her muscles twitched deliciously, and she loved the thick feel of him, keeping her grounded, so totally there with her. What would it be like when he was no longer there with her?

She could tell he was close to losing control. His heavy muscles were heaving with the exertion, sweat was gathering on his beautiful brow. With the evening light streaming through the window, he was a beautiful golden bronze, and his eyes glowed like blue flames burning low.

His curved lips were tight in concentration as he started working her toward another orgasm. Each in and out was sheer torture, in the most delicious way. He was so huge that almost every move made her feel she couldn't possibly hold him, then when he came inside, she felt so fully stretched, so fully stimulated, that it was almost an out of body experience. And then she'd look at his face, so cut, so handsome, so intent on her pleasure and almost tender in his focus, and she'd relax and just feel the pleasure of his embrace. The wondrous feel of him hitting the g-spot each time he moved, the way his finger played against her, bringing her toward another incredible orgasm.

She held her breath as it happened again, wondering at how she could feel so good and so awful at the same time. It was the most intense pleasure she'd ever known, but it was like tasting the most divine air only to know you'd never breathe it again. Wouldn't it have been better not to know? Her body didn't think so, as wave after wave of pleasure assaulted her senses, melting her to a little blob that wanted to cling to him and never let go.

His eyes burned as he watched her and his arms trembled. What was going on behind that stern, focused expression? She felt like her face told him everything. Her agony, her ecstasy, each tremor of hot pleasure. But his face hid so much.

She wanted to see him lose it, wanted to see him come apart. She started to thrust against him, locking her ankles behind him and rising to meet him, increasing the speed even as he cursed and tried to slow them. He reached between them again and rubbed the sensitive nub that was still aching for his touch even after two explosive orgasms. He worked it quickly, savagely, determined to give her another orgasm before she could get him off and end everything. They fought a battle for pleasure for one another, and neither had ever experienced anything so exhilarating.

He won, and she cursed as she threw her head back in pleasure. She bit back a scream as her body shuddered within her, as white hot heat spread through her in waves. From her fingertips to her toes to the very top of her scalp, she was so alive and aware of him. She never wanted this to end.

But she wanted to see him go. Wanted to see her stern sea captain cry out her name on a hoarse shoat. Somehow she knew just how he'd sound. She wanted to make him do it for the rest of her life. Wanted their bears to run together. Could hear the wild part of her howling for satisfaction, to see her mate pleased completely.

She drove harder against him, taking him deep inside her and enjoying the pained but pleasured look on his face as his blue eyes met hers, looking as roiled as an angry ocean. He might be trying to look calm, but he was definitely feeling something intense behind those sea-blue eyes. Something cosmic and eternal just like she was feeling.

She could almost count the thrusts it would take. But his finger moved between them to take her with him. Three. Two. One. She heard his hoarse shout just as pleasure rippled through her in her final release for the night. Through the intense sensation, she struggled to look up at him. His muscles tensed and his tremendous arms went rigid. His features went slightly soft as he called her name.

He was the most beautiful man she'd ever seen, and she loved the feel of him jerking inside of her, spilling his seed into the protection between them. He was so warm, so strong, and she longed to wrap herself in his arms.

He seemed to hear her silent request and fell against her, shielding her with his huge body as his orgasm finished. Then he quickly pulled out and grabbed a small towel he must have carried in from the bathroom and put it between them. Then he stayed over her, shaking slightly, like what had just happened had impacted him as much as it had impacted her.

And it had impacted her down to her core.

He was so heavy, so huge, but he was a welcome weight and she wrapped her arms around him and let her heart swell with joy just at having him so close. It didn't matter that she'd barely known him. It didn't matter that they were from different worlds and had different temperaments.

He was her bear, and it would hurt like hell to ever be apart from him.

She tried to keep tears from falling, but it was fruitless. She knew he heard her sniffles when he sat up and stared down at her.

"Kim," he said softly, looking at her with wonder, looking just as devastated as she felt. "I can't do this to us anymore."

Her heart was cold at his words but she knew he was right. She sat up slightly as he rolled off her to sit at her side, still wrapping himself in a towel. He still looked magnificent, with bronzed, heavy shoulders and perfect, rippling abs. Bear shifters were known for being large and he was no exception. His beautiful hair was coming loose from it's ponytail and softening his face.

When he wasn't angry, he was almost angelically beautiful. Maybe that was why he tried to look so stern. But given his build and his sense of presence, she doubted there was anyone who wouldn't be scared of him if he wanted them to be.

She leaned in against him, and he stiffened but allowed it. "We've really done it now, right?" she asked. "I mean, we're wholly unsuitable, but—"

He cut her off with a gentle touch to her lips, and then put an arm around her and drew her close. They stayed like that as the sun finished setting. She could hear the gentle beating of his heart and she grinned against it. She loved that heartbeat.

They were so different, but she knew that in other circumstances, that would have just made it fun to get to know each other. He could have taught her about life on a ship, she could have encouraged him to go on more adventures. It would have been amazing.

She wondered if he was having similar thoughts. "What now?" she asked.

"I said you could have my nights," he said. "But I don't think I can do that anymore. I'm already…we're getting…" He .shoved a hand angrily through his hair. "I can't do it."

"Getting attached," she said. "I know." She didn't say the word *mate*. She didn't need to. The way he was acting, so possessive, so warm, given what a cold and distant man he was usually, told her everything she needed to know.

He was amazing. He was everything that could make her happy. She knew there was only one way that either of them could let this go.

"Tell me why you can't commit," she said.

His lips tightened. "I don't want to talk about it now."

"At least maybe if we each knew why the other couldn't be with us, we could have some closure."

His arm tightened around her. "I don't want closure. I just want to pretend this won't end. I'll tell you why I can't be with you when we have to say goodbye. Right now I just want to pretend this can go on forever."

She sighed deeply and relaxed against him, watching the beautiful water that looked purplish under the night sky with little ribbons of whitish yellow from the bright moon lighting the clouds. She had enjoyed law school and practicing law, but she'd never felt the soul deep satisfaction that she did here, on this island with her mate.

Maybe something in the universe really set mates up so that shifters could be happier with their mate than they ever could have thought to be alone. Maybe that was why she'd been drawn to the Caymans and gotten dive certified.

But why did she have to be drawn in when it didn't even matter?

"So, you'll tell me when you say goodbye?" she asked, placing a hand on his chest and making slow circles and enjoying the way it made his breathing speed up before he removed her hand and gave her a playful glare.

She let her hand rest.

"I'll tell you then, and I hope you'll tell me," he said.

"Why?" she asked.

"Because it's the only way I'll be able to let you go." He leaned his head on top of hers. They couldn't have been more different, but they also couldn't have been more right for each other. "That's why we can't keep doing this. Each time we do this, I'm becoming a little more joined with you, a little more of me is soldered to you and I know I'll never get it back. If you rip any more away of me when you leave, I'll be a shell of a person. It might already be too late. But yes, when we have our final goodbye, we'll tell each other our reasons, and we'll take it from there."

"What do we do in the meantime, then?" she asked. "Ignore each other?"

"No," he said, teasing her braids. "In the meantime I'll take you around the island on the boat tours we have scheduled. I don't want to let you out of my sight. I just can't make love to you again. It…takes too much of me."

She nodded, an ache settling deep in her throat. She felt the same, but she didn't think she could have decided not to have sex as easily as he did. She hoped that maybe they could do it one more time before she left. She craved it like she craved fresh air after a year underground.

"Sebastien?" she asked, needing to lighten the mood.

"Yes?"

"I enjoyed hoisting your mainsail," she teased, looking up to see him raising an eyebrow. She almost expected a stern retort or for him to glare at her. She wasn't expecting him to grin widely and tease her back.

"And I enjoyed shivering your timbers," he said. When she gasped in offense, he tickled her until they were down under the covers. Then they rested their heads on the pillows and watched each other until sleep claimed Kim first, and then Sebastien, who put his hand over Kim's before falling asleep.

CHAPTER 9

The rest of the week passed far too fast. So many fun moments with Sebastien, even at times she was just watching him from across the deck.

She loved the way his hair whipped in the wind. The way he was so stern but saved secretive smiles for her.

She didn't know how she was going to leave him. Even though they hadn't made love since that night in his suite, she'd felt her love for him growing, her need for him growing.

She still hoped to talk him into just one more night together if she could. Even if it hurt, it would give her just one more dose of what she needed from him.

Perhaps even more than that though, she craved knowing

what was holding him back.

Over the past week, when she'd laughed in his arms or swam beside him in the water, she'd found her resolve weakening. Found herself not wanting to do what her family wanted.

She knew it was dishonorable of her. Knew that if she called her family to ask for quarter, they wouldn't understand. Her father had been obsessed with having shifter grandchildren since he'd had his own children, and there was apparently a family in New York that felt the same.

Still, she was a grown woman. She could make her own choices. What could they really do to her if she didn't?

Disown her. The thought was painful to the bear in her, but not as painful as the thought of losing her mate. She loved her family. Without them she'd never have gotten through law school, and without her dad's firm, she'd never have found a job so quickly.

But somehow, not being able to practice law seemed to be a small price to pay in order to stay here with Sebastien.

But how did he feel about it? She looked over at him as he unloaded the luggage from their most recent boat trip. He'd taken over as captain but she'd still had ample excuse to spend time with him, and he no longer seemed to mind it. He'd changed so much from the surly man who had stomped away from his boat when threatened with relaxation and removed from his command.

She stifled a grin as he helped an older woman carry her luggage up the dock. She frowned when the woman checked out her mate's ass. Oh well, she could look as long as she didn't touch.

Wait, who was Kim kidding? She'd be gone in a few days and it wouldn't matter what she did after that. She wrapped her hands around herself and paced on the deck of the yacht they'd gone on that day.

Sebastien had promised her one last boat ride tonight after things wrapped up.

Tomorrow she'd be packing and saying goodbye to the other women and heading out to stay two nights on the other side of Grand Cayman.

It'd be a good chance to clear her head before going home.

Sebastien waved as he walked back toward her. He jumped easily up on deck and gave her a swift hug before checking to see that no on was watching. As he had a habit of doing lately, he pulled back and looked down at her face intently, trying to gauge if she was doing okay.

She was. Sort of.

"Why don't you go get some dinner and a break?" he said. "I have a few things to do before we head out tonight."

She nodded. "Sounds good." She wanted to stay with him but figured he needed a break to clean up and get ready to go. Maybe even to get emotionally ready.

She squeezed his hand and jumped lightly off the deck and onto the dock, which swayed slightly in the wind.

She gave him a last, suspicious look as he stood watching her, a slight gleam in his eyes and his hands clasped behind his back, displaying his magnificent arms and chest.

She shook her head and walked down the dock. Not sure what to make of it all. Just a few more days, her heart told her. Then it's just like ripping off a bandage.

A really terrible bandage.

***

Sebastien hauled the cooler that had his surprise for Kim onto the ship just as the sun began to set. He raised a hand to shade his eyes and looked out over the dock for her approach.

A sensuous figure in a carefully wrapped sarong was making her way down the dock. A little chill ran up his spine in anticipation. He couldn't believe he'd ever been annoyed by her. Now his body ached with tension whenever it knew she was coming near. His bear was constantly at a low growl, buzzing within his chest, and he had fallen into a habit of rubbing it absentmindedly when it became too much to deal with.

He couldn't believe this was their last night together. He was glad they would each know what was holding the other back, but he also knew it wouldn't change anything.

His father had known he wanted his mate. He had married her, mated her, but it hadn't changed anything. Despite the animals inside one another wanting what they wanted, it hadn't been enough.

No matter what was holding Kim back, eventually she'd decide it wasn't enough, and she'd leave him, like his mother had. And he couldn't bear it.

Not again.

Not to mention how much worse this would be. No, if it was going to hurt now, it was only a fraction of how much it would hurt later. He wanted to trust her, like his dad had trusted his mom, but he also couldn't.

All he could remember was the sting of having someone he loved, someone he depended on, suddenly gone, and the empty ache that had sent him running to the ocean and a grumpy ship captain who had taken him under his wing and taught him about the sea to distract him.

The sea was always there for him. He could always come back to it. His family thought he was the cold one, the distant one, but perhaps he was really the most sensitive, the most hurt by their mother's abandonment, because he was definitely the one most held back by it.

But he was grateful for the chance he'd gotten to know his mate. There was something wonderful between them and he was glad they'd had a chance to explore it. And it would hurt to say goodbye, but then the sting would fade. Hopefully.

He reached out a hand as she reached him. Her braids were woven into one thick braid and rested over her shoulder alluringly. Her curves looked amazing beneath the intricate wrap of the soft sarong that fluttered slightly in the wind. He licked his finger, put it up in the air and grinned. "Good wind."

"Good," she said, laughing slightly as he helped her up onto the deck.

Tonight he was taking her out on his private boat. A smaller yacht, with just a small cabin below only big enough for two. But he didn't plan to take her downstairs with him tonight. He knew if he did that, he wouldn't be able to let her go. And if he didn't, she'd blame him for the rest of their lives.

They had both agreed on no quarter, no begging, no rule changes, and they were about to find out why. But first, he had a surprise.

"Come here," he said, guiding her to a seat next to his. He untied them from the dock, pulled the bumpers that kept his boat from scratching, turned on the lights that helped him steer as the sun was fading, and started the boat.

It rumbled to life with a satisfying growl and he moved the throttle back to pull away from the dock. He palmed the wheel, aware she was watching him, that it turned her on to see him handle the boat like he did.

She liked him being in control almost as much as he liked being in control. Another reason they would have been fantastic mates, had things been different.

He still laughed inside when he thought about that first

day together, after she'd stolen his boat. And their first night, in the dark in a dinghy, and the night in his suite. And they had so many memories to add after that.

They drove out until the shore and the resort were distant and they had the distinct feeling of being alone on the ocean, rocked by the waves. He dropped the anchor. Looking at the sun, he guessed they still had forty-five minutes of daylight, at least.

He laid out a quilted blanket and opened the cooler to reveal Dom Perignon champagne and strawberry. He popped the cork on the champagne and let it spill off the side of the boat, then brought it over to her and poured her a glass. When he handed it to her, she grinned, but he thought it looked slightly pained, and he didn't like that.

"Only the best for you New York types," he said.

"I didn't know you had such luxury out here," she teased.

"We aren't complete savages," he said, taking a strawberry out of the container and placing it gently between her lips. She took another sip and chewed and swallowed with pure rapture in her face. Damn, he wanted to do that again. So he did.

The sunset was gorgeous, all orange and red and pink and fading blue, with the water getting brighter toward the horizon as it flashed back the colors of the sky it was reflecting. He didn't think he'd ever had a more perfect moment.

"Sebastien?" she asked quietly, feeding him a strawberry and giving him a moment's excuse not to answer.

He chewed slowly and then swallowed. The bite of the sour berry tingled with the tang of the champagne. It felt a little like their relationship. Sweet but bitter. So bitter. "Yes?"

"Do you want to go first or should I?"

"Should we even do this?" he blurted out. "I mean, it won't change anything. It's just going to make us angry at one another, if the reasons aren't good enough."

"No, because we both agreed to what we agreed to," she said.

He gritted his teeth. He guessed what really worried him is that if she didn't have a good enough reason, then his reason would also be faulty, and then he'd end up risking everything for her. And when he thought of that, sheer panic welled up inside him. It felt like he couldn't breathe. It was even worse than the thought of losing her.

He swallowed and set his glass aside. "I can go first if you want."

"Or I can," she said.

"I'll go," he said. "Before I lose my nerve."

"Ha, you? The brave sea captain, losing his nerve? Impossible," she teased.

"Come sit with me," he said, moving to the back. There was a soft bench there and they could watch the sunset together. For a long moment, they sat there quietly.

"I'm a polar bear," he said.

"I guessed," she said. "There's just something fierce and arctic about you. But how do you live out here in the warmth?"

"As well as any creature, as long as there is water. And as long as we don't put on the heavy coat of fat that helps us survive in cold climates."

"Ah," she said, running a hand over his hard abdomen. "Not much chance of that happening."

"My dad met my mom and it was love at first sight. Fated mates, if you know what that is." He felt stupid right after saying it. Of course she knew what that was. *They* were fated mates. They were just ignoring it, which, now that he thought about it, didn't seem smart.

But anyway…

"They had three of us, which was astonishing, because bear shifters aren't very fertile. But they were both strong alphas, and I suppose that helped."

She nodded, letting him continue without interruption. He sort of wished she *would* interrupt. He hadn't really talked about this with anyone.

"Anyway, she hated the cold. She and my dad would argue when I was little, but she was good to us. A good mom. And then one day, she was just gone."

Her face tightened. He was used to seeing her smiling and lighthearted, so it was quite a striking change.

"What do you mean gone? Weren't they mated?"

He nodded. "It destroyed my dad. I don't think he ever considered the possibility, even though he knew they were very different."

Realization dawned on her and her eyes widened. "So, you think that because we're different, I'm going to be like her and leave you?"

He bit his lip. That did sound bad. But he would bet that if you had asked his mom back when his parents were first dating

143

if she would leave her mate, she'd have said it was ridiculous as well. "They were different. Too different. At first, the mating thrall was enough to keep her beside him…but after some time."

"Sebastien, I wouldn't leave you. I love you."

He felt the hardness in his face. Felt the cold inside him rise to the surface. "And you think she didn't?"

She shut her mouth, eyes troubled. "I don't know what would make a woman leave her cubs. I don't understand that at all. At the same time, who am I to judge? But are you just going to judge every woman based on one who did something really heinous?"

"I learned something as a child that I don't seem to be able to unlearn as an adult. There's something very cold in me, and I'm not sure how to change it. I just know that I'd rather let you go now than watch you walk away when you'll devastate me and our children."

Her eyes widened. "I'm a little offended that you think I'm that irresponsible," she said.

He tried to crack a smile. "Well, you did steal my boat when I first met you."

She tried to smile back. "I suppose."

He put his hands together and tried to look casual. "Besides, what does it matter? You have your own reasons for leaving."

She tightened her lips into a line. "Yes, but it'd be much easier to leave if I knew that one day, you'd trust someone enough to let them make you happy."

He frowned. "Why?"

She shook her head. "Haven't you been happy these past few days?"

He nodded emphatically. No use hiding that.

"You could be happy again."

"No," he said. She was his mate. She was the only one worth risking it all for, and he still couldn't do it. The trauma was too strong. And she would find someone else before he could beat it.

It was okay. It had to be.

"Tell me yours," he said.

She seemed to be holding back tears, and he felt like an ass. He didn't know how to make it clear it was about him, not about her. She was a good woman. If she found someone compatible, she probably had a chance at something long term, not a fling like what they had.

"I'm betrothed," she said. "Well, I will be when I get home."

"Do you know your fiancé?" he asked.

"No," she said. "I didn't want to know. Not when I was planning to come here and do whatever I wanted."

"Do your friends know about us?" he asked. "Or about this fiance?"

She shook her head. "No. They know I'm infatuated with you, but I let them think you were playing hard to get and I was chasing other males."

His jaw tightened. "Why?"

"Because if anyone sees how much I already love you, I think I'll break," she said. "I can go through with this, but I just can't stand for anyone to watch me do it. If I pretend it's all some big joke, just some fling, then it's fine. But it's not, you're my mate, and for the first time in my life, I want to go against my family. My family, who has been so good to me. But even if I did, you wouldn't come with me, would you? You wouldn't take a risk on me, because you're sure I would leave you?"

She stood and jerked her hand away when he tried to stop her. "And I just don't understand why you would let something so small stop you."

He gritted his teeth together. It didn't feel small.

"I mean, I've known this would happen since I was a child. If I tried to walk away from this, I'd literally betray everyone who has ever cared about me. I'd lose everything, and I'd be breaking my word." She looked at him with narrowed eyes.

He frowned. "What do you want from me?" he asked. "You should keep your word." He saw the hurt in her eyes as he said it, but he knew even if he fought for it, even if he ignored the coldness inside him, one day she would resent him for making her do something that would make her turn on her family.

It was even more reason why she would one day turn on him and leave. He couldn't do it.

"If I was willing to turn my back on them, would you accept me? Would you even try to battle your demons?" she asked. "Would you trust me?"

He considered the question in his heart, trying to ignore the low growling of his bear that was getting louder every second. What could he honestly say? Other than the mating instinct within him, there was no reason they would work, nothing that would hold her here as he worked long days on the ocean.

She wouldn't just be giving up her family, but her home in New York, and her occupation as lawyer, which she had presumably spent years in school for.

Perhaps if she'd had nothing to lose, he could have made a play for them, could have hoped she'd stay. But she had everything waiting for her, so what would stop her from going once she tired of him? Once he wasn't an adventure anymore.

Eventually, his sternness would get to her. She was like a feather floating on the wind and he was like a rock stuck at the bottom of the ocean.

Trapped.

He realized that while he'd been thinking, he'd given her all the answer she'd expected. Hurt flared in her eyes. This was everything he'd been trying to avoid. Everything that they could have avoided if they'd just not gotten involved.

But trying to cut things off with her had been like trying to stop falling after you've already jumped off the cliff. Impossible.

He'd just wanted their last night together to be pleasant. But he could see now he had been naive.

"I should take you home, shouldn't I?" he said.

She nodded, he could see the tightness in the way she held herself, head high, throat tensed, arms folded over her beautiful chest. Damn, she was gorgeous.

But he'd be able to forget her someday, wouldn't he?

He packed things up while she sat stiffly on the bench, watching the sea, which was becoming navy blue in the darkness. The sun was gone, and the moon was out, and he used the lights on the front of the boat to guide them back to the dock.

Coldness rose in him as they got closer, and he didn't think it was just the coldness of the night. It felt like he was making a colossal mistake, and as he helped her get off the boat and unloaded things, it felt like it was harder and harder to breath. He followed her down the dock in silence, watching her hips sway in front of him.

"Why won't they let you choose?" he asked. "Why are you

going to let someone arrange a marriage for you when you're a fully grown woman?" he asked.

"I'm also a shifter," she said. "And our kind is dying out."

"But why the person they chose?"

"We've been promised from birth," she said sadly.

"That's some bullshit," he said, catching her hand. "Why someone like him and not me?"

She looked into his eyes in surprise. "Do you want it to be you?"

He hesitated. That was a mistake. She pulled her hand away and kept walking. He grabbed her by the hand and pulled her against him, hard. Then he crushed his mouth down on hers, hoping to kiss her in a way she would never forget.

He'd kiss the sense out of her and make her forget anything existed in New York. He'd keep her here with him against the odds.

She struggled slightly and then pulled away, wiping her mouth. "Don't do that," she said.

"Fine," he said hoarsely.

She watched him for a moment with narrowed eyes, then

came in again, grabbed his shirt to yank him down and crushed her mouth over his. "Asshole," she murmured against his lips. "Coward," she gasped, as he stroked his tongue against her and stifled any more words she might have said. He didn't want the last words between them to be cruel.

Heat moved through him as they kissed, and when they finally pulled away, he saw the same heat reflected in her eyes. He sort of wished they could just rewind the whole week, and she could steal his boat again, and they could have one more week away from reality.

"So even if I was willing to walk away from my responsibilities, you wouldn't fight for me?" she asked.

His face tightened. He didn't know. He was suddenly faced with what-ifs that he hadn't considered. He hadn't asked himself what he would do if she was willing to let go of her reasons. He wasn't a man who could make an easy decision even when it was presented to him. He had to think.

She took it wrong. "I have my answer."

"Wait," he said, trying to follow her as she started to run away from him, over the sand. She had only asked what if, she hadn't said she was willing to stay. It wasn't fair of her to do that. This couldn't be the end for them. "Kim, don't leave things like this."

She turned back to him with fury in her eyes, and then weariness. "Honestly, Sebastien. I'd rather leave things like this. It'll make it easier to leave you."

CHAPTER 10

Kim's words hit him like a cannonball to his heart, deadening it with an intense blast. When she was out of sight, he sat down on the sand and watched the ocean warily.

Why were things so much simpler out there?

He stayed there for an interminable amount of time, and then only realized what he was doing when he felt a rough tap at his shoulder.

"What are you doing out here?" A low voice asked.

He looked up to see his brother Scott. The businessman among them. The one who took care of the hotel. Scott had a habit of patrolling the beaches to make sure the guests were all in and safe, but he seemed to be even more agitated than usual tonight.

"Do you ever think about our mother?" Sebastien asked.

Scott plopped in the sand beside him. "How could I not? I try not to dwell on it though."

"I mean. We watched it wreck our dad, and we were left alone. I think it would have been different if we'd known where she went or what happened to her," he said. "But she just vanished."

"Yeah," Scott said.

"Do you remember how he screamed?" Sebastien said.

"Yes. It was like she was dead."

"Except she'd left him on purpose, which is almost worse."

"I'm sure he wouldn't have wanted anything to happen to her."

Sebastien thought of that. He knew that he wouldn't want anything to happen to Kim. "Do you think he's still angry?"

Scott considered it. Scott was the thoughtful one in the family. The rational one. Sebastien liked to pretend he was rational, but he was finding he was also more emotional than he thought.

"Maybe you should ask him," Scott said.

That made sense. He'd never spoken to his dad about what happened. He was a grown man now, and he'd never really forgiven his father for choosing someone who would hurt them all like that. He guessed part of what bothered him most was how much it had hurt his father.

He stood and brushed the sand off his knees, a new sense of purpose flooding him. "I'm going to go talk to him," he said.

"Wish my problems were that easily solvable," Scott muttered.

"Oh? What's the problem," he asked.

Scott shook his head. "Nothing."

"He paired you up with that artist lady, didn't he? She a handful?"

Scott grinned. "Yes, in the best way."

"Still, storm brewing?"

"Yes," Scott said. "Sailor take warning."

"I don't understand those artistic types," Sebastien said, folding his arms.

155

"Who does?" Scott said. "All I know is business and running this hotel."

"And you do a fantastic job of it," Sebastien said.

Scott leaned back on his arms, a faint smile on his face. "Do you know, I don't think you've ever paid me a compliment on it before. I think Kim is making an impression on you."

Sebastien felt his face color and was glad for the darkness to hide it. He wanted to talk to his brother, but a part of him ached at being away from Kim.

"Kim is Mara's cousin you know. Mara being the artist," Scott said.

"I wish I could stay here and help you like you helped me," Sebastien said hesitantly. "But I don't understand women."

"Who does?" Scott said, standing and helping his brother up. "Don't worry about it. What are big brothers for?"

"Beating up men who come to take our brother's mate?" he asked.

Scott grinned. They'd had to detain a certain bear the week before, after it had tried to kidnap their youngest brother's mate. It hadn't taken long.

"Yeah, that's one of the funner jobs," Scott said, laughing.

Sebastien looked into his brother's eyes and saw a solidarity he'd been missing. He really had been closed off, and Kim had been opening him up. Now he'd open up a little further, talk to his dad, and see if there wasn't room in his heart for a little more trust.

***

Kim stomped back to her room. She couldn't believe the cold look in Sebastien's eyes. She'd been offering him something she didn't even believe she had the strength to offer until that moment, and he hadn't even said anything. Just stared at her with that cold gaze that said she should already know the answer. And of course, he'd had to kiss her like that.

She was angry. She was angry in a way she hadn't known she was angry but she was feeling very keenly for the first time in her life. She'd hidden in her adventures and her fun and her studies and her job and her family, but a part of her was damned angry.

When she got to her room, she picked up her phone, stared at it, willed herself to call on it, and then chucked it aside. What would she say?

How was she going to tell her dad that she wasn't going to be the good girl she'd always promised to be? She looked in the mirror and saw the face of a grown woman who didn't want to be a child anymore. Didn't want to do what her parents asked. And yet, the draw to please them was still strong.

But so was the draw to go back to Sebastien, chain herself to his side and make him see she'd never leave him.

But that wasn't where they were at. He didn't even want her, it seemed.

She paced in the room and looked at the phone, and then a knock came on the door.

She strode to it wearily and opened to see Wilson. He was wearing board shorts in bright blue and pink and a white tee shirt with a logo on it in the same colors. He looked slightly ridiculous, but pleasant as usual.

And pleasant was just what she was in the mood for. "What can I do for you?"

He cocked his head and looked in at the room. "Did I come at a bad time? You seem upset."

She shrugged. "I'm fine."

He pushed his way into the room and she let him. The other girls would probably be home soon. She sat in one of the chairs and put her feet up, feeling restless. He sat on the couch across from her, looking thoughtful, and then leaned over to hand her something he'd pulled from his shirt pocket.

It was a worn picture of her. Her heart beat double time in her chest as she looked at it. "What does this mean?"

"I'm the one your family wants you to be with," he said, giving her a rueful grin. "I came out to see what you were like. I was hoping we could get to know each other before we were paired up. As if that would make things less awkward."

She swallowed. She'd been an idiot, and she felt bad for brushing him off. But she just couldn't see anyone but Sebastien.

"It's the sea captain, right?" Wilson asked, looking sad as he tucked the photo away again. "I can tell by the way you look at him. Honestly, I think it's stupid that our parents thought we could do things the way wolves do. We're bears. We're different."

She nodded. "I don't know. I imagine there are some arranged wolf shifter matings that don't go as planned either."

He nodded. "I'll say no to the engagement for you, if you want," he said. "I'm not a monster. I don't want a mate who hates me. I want one who values me."

She looked him over. He was strong and handsome. "What kind of bear are you?" she asked.

"Grizzly, like you," he said. He was tall and buff. He hadn't ever done anything wrong. She wished the bear inside her wasn't tearing at her to go to Sebastien, whom she was sure was her mate.

"I'm sorry," he said. "That I couldn't win you over."

"You shouldn't have to win someone over," she said. "You deserve someone who's excited about you."

"And the sea captain? Is he excited about you?"

"He has commitment issues," she muttered.

Wilson thought that over. "What about if we made a deal then?" he asked. "What if you come out on a boat trip with me? One I charter, and we try to get to know each other. Just us together," he said. "And if it doesn't work, I'll call it off. Then your family can't get mad."

"What if they do?" she asked.

He gave her a frank look that she felt laid her bare. "Then do you really fucking care?" he asked.

She shook her head. "No, I really fucking don't." She was tired of caring. And maybe a fun day on a boat with Wilson would make her forget the pain she was feeling from Sebastien not wanting her. Maybe it would give him time to come to his senses. But she doubted it.

He'd made it clear from the first time they'd been together that he wasn't looking for more time.

"Don't make that face," Wilson said. "I can't stand when females are sad. Tell you what, why don't you pack and get some rest, and we'll head out tomorrow morning?"

She nodded and yawned. Rest would be good. So would a day on the ocean away from her infuriating pirate. She said goodnight to Wilson and closed the door behind him.

***

Sebastien waited for his father to pour the scotch he was

holding, but his dad hesitated and then set the glass bottle down. He sat in his chair and clasped his hands together in front of him, leaning forward to face Sebastien.

It was like looking at his future. His dad's eyes were slightly paler, his blond hair was dotted with white and gray, and he had lines around his mouth and eyes from years of living. From years of pain.

There was nothing worse in the shifter world than separation from one's mate.

His dad studied him for a moment, and then spoke. "I should have talked to you sooner about your mom," he said. "You grew up so quickly. Always around the boats. Always away from shore when you weren't at school. You were such a quiet, intense kid that I didn't know what to say. I guess because you weren't as outwardly expressive, I thought maybe nothing was wrong. But I can see that was a futile hope. Wishful thinking on my part maybe."

He saw a familiar look of pain in his dad's eyes and stood to pour him a drink. He poured another for himself and handed the first to his dad.

His dad raised it up and looked at the scotch like he didn't know what to make of it. It shimmered in the light as he held it. He took a sip, grimaced, and set it back on the table.

"I think though, the only thing I would have wanted to tell you, and that I'm glad I have a chance to tell you now, is that I don't regret it."

Sebastien's heart thumped. "What?"

"I don't regret it."

"But you were in agony," Sebastien said, noting for the first time how similar his deep voice was to that of his father's.

"I don't regret it," his father repeated. "Even if she couldn't love me, even if she couldn't stay, she gave me you boys. The light of my life," he said.

Sebastien frowned. His father had never spoken like this. And he was far too old to go back and play catch with him or rewrite his childhood. His father hadn't been present. His mother had left. But he had somehow become a man all the same. One that took care of others. One that Kim wanted.

Just the mention of her name stung.

"Your mother and I were an odd case. But even with how it turned out, fate seemed to know better than us. All I want is to see you and your brothers happy with mates. To know that I didn't ruin it for you."

Sebastien grunted. "Well, Sky's already happy."

"And good for him," Sam said, shaking his head. "But what about you Sebastien? If I'm not mistaken, there's a woman that really loves you somewhere in the building."

Sebastien nodded. "She's promised to another."

"Would she be if she thought you were an option?"

"It would alienate her from her family. Even if she weren't the type to leave, that would eventually force her to."

"I think that's her decision to make," Sam said, propping his feet on the table between them and studying his son. "I guess there's really only one thing you need to consider."

"What?" Sebastien asked, trying to keep his expression neutral.

"Whether you can really let her go."

Sebastien felt the panic from before rising within him, threatening to cut off his breath.

"Can you let another man make her happy?" his father pressed.

No.

"Can you let another man take her to bed?"

Hell no.

"Can you let another man give her cubs?"

Fuck no.

"Then go get her," his dad said.

"It's not that simple," he said. "There's her family. We're from different worlds." *She could hurt me.*

His dad gave him a wry grin and set his drink down. "Or maybe it is that simple. We're bears, son."

Sebastien's bear roared inside him and he put a hand to his ringing head. His father was right, he would have to fight for Kim.

It was the dumb thing to do, but what did he know? He was just a stupid bear, stupidly in love with a mate that might not stay and might not want him.

And he meant to go and get her all the same.

He waved absently at his dad and then walked out of the hotel room. He went down to the lobby and strode around in the wide space, trying to gather his thoughts.

He was shocked when one of the customers from his earlier boat trip stopped him with a hand on his arm. He raised to his full height to glare down at the man but stopped when the man smiled and pulled his hand back.

"Sorry man, just saying goodbye," he said.

"What was your name again?" Sebastien asked, trying not to sound grumpy.

"Wilson," he said.

Ah, that did sound familiar. Right, he was the one that had made him jealous on his first trip with Kim. "Right, Wilson. What can I do for you?"

"Nothing," the other man said, putting his hands smoothly in his pockets. "Just wanted to thank you for taking good care of my fiancé."

His heart thudded to a stop. "What?"

Wilson shrugged. "I know it's a little weird, but I wanted to meet her before it was final."

"And is it final?" he asked, trying not to sound like he cared too much.

Wilson studied him. The handsome, smooth man seemed

to possess more sense than Sebastien had initially thought because he seemed to sense that there was something between him and Kim.

"It could be," Wilson said. "I'm taking her out on my boat tomorrow. Hoping to mate her if possible, before she changes her mind."

"Like hell," Sebastien snarled, grabbing the other man by his collar and hauling him off his feet to dangle in the air. The other man grinned at him incorrigibly and he had to set him down.

Wilson exhaled with a cough and then straightened his shirt. "Easy big guy. All I did was ask her. Why would she say yes if she didn't want me?"

Because I was an asshole who made her feel unwanted, he thought. But of course he wasn't going to say that out loud. Not to this jackass who had designs on his woman. His mate. Damn, it felt good to acknowledge it. He didn't know how this whole thing was going to work, but he felt better than he had in forever just knowing that he was going for it. That he wasn't going to let fear hold him back.

Wilson was still studying him, and he realized that if the man really was his enemy, he wouldn't have let him know about their plans.

"When are you leaving?" he asked.

"Seven," Wilson said.

He laughed. "If you can even get her up then."

"She's pretty determined," Wilson said, frowning. "In fact, I'm not sure you'll even be able to convince her not to go. Not as you are now, anyway." He grinned at Sebastien and put his hands behind his head to stroll away. "But that's your problem to figure out. Not mine."

Sebastien growled but the other man had already turned the corner and disappeared out of sight. She might not want him, hm? Maybe not as he was. But as he stared at the gift stop, and a costumed mannequin standing at the entrance, an idea came to mine.

He had an idea how she *would* accept him.

It was time for some plundering.

CHAPTER 11

Kim's heart ached as she stared out at the water. It seemed so empty without Sebastien. Even though someone was driving the boat, and Wilson was standing nearby, commenting on the beauty of the weather, she felt incredibly cold inside. Like she'd made a bad mistake.

"Maybe we should go back," she said. She didn't know what would change when she got there. Sebastien still wouldn't be willing to give her a chance. But maybe she'd finally be willing to confront her family about what she didn't want to do. Hopefully she'd be able to keep her job at the law firm, but if not, she was capable. Hopefully she could find something else.

She tapped her fingers on the railing, waiting for Wilson's

response.

"I could take you back," he said, leaning on the railing and looking out. "But I have a feeling it's about to be a moot point."

Her gaze snapped to where he was looking and she saw a boat coming toward them in the distance.

Holy shit.

It was Sebastien, or at least she thought it was. He was standing tall behind the wheel as he drove toward her, and there was a flag mounted at the back of the boat where one would normally mount a water ski tower.

Her mouth twitched. It was a pirate flag.

She squinted to see him more clearly, and as he came into view, she could tell he was wearing different clothes. Specifically, a ridiculous looking pirate hat and ruffled white shirt that looked suspiciously familiar.

Damn, had he actually stolen clothes from the gift shop mannequin? And why was he coming all the way out here?

Her heart sped up as he got closer, and Wilson came beside her to put his arm around her shoulder.

"What is he doing here?" she asked, looking at him accusingly. "Who told him?"

Wilson shrugged. "No idea. I feel betrayed." But as he folded his arms and looked out at the approaching vessel, she thought that he looked anything but.

Why would he willingly give her away? Well, it didn't matter. Sebastien was actually coming for her, and she had Wilson to thank. She put a hand on his shoulder. "I'm sorry it couldn't work out. Really I am."

"That's okay," he said. "It gives me a chance to find my own mate as well."

"And if you don't?" she asked.

"Life is full of risks," he said cryptically. "Good luck with your family. I'll cry off but I doubt that'll get you off the hook."

She nodded. She didn't care. She shouldn't have known from the start that she wasn't strong enough to walk away from her mate. It was pure natural instinct, and it felt delicious to even consider it.

"Ahoy!" A deep voice boomed. Despite his ridiculous attire, he looked stern as usual. The mannequin's outfit was too small for him, but it only made his bulging muscles look that much more attractive.

She could tell from his narrowed eyes as he watched her appraise him that he was feeling ridiculous, but he'd done this for her. For *her*. And that meant everything. It made her think they could beat the odds, that she could be strong enough to move on and leave the past she'd worked so hard for behind.

But she still had to wait to see what he had to say.

"Avast!" he shouted in that low, husky voice that drove her crazy. "Permission to come aboard."

Wilson laughed.

"Never mind! Permission not needed to come aboard!" Sebastien boomed, seeming to remember that pirates didn't need to be polite. He had bumpers tied on the side of his boat so that he could come close to Wilson's smaller vessel without scratching it. Then he looped a rope around the railing of Wilson's, and then used his powerful arms to haul him up and onto their ship.

She took a step backward. Even in that ridiculous costume, he was intimidating. So tall, with that golden hair whipping in the wind. He was wearing black boots that gleamed in the sun. He looked a little too hot.

She was wearing a swimsuit with a sundress over it, and she felt hot as he studied her slowly, raking his eyes over her. She wanted to laugh and melt at the same time. If someone had told her that the grumpy ship captain who didn't want anything to do with her would be acquiescing to her pirate fantasy, she would have thought they were out of their minds.

But here he was.

She took a step back, not sure what to say.

"I'm here for the booty," he said in a low voice.

She stifled a laugh and looked at Wilson. How Sebastien could say something in such a serious tone when it was so ridiculous, she didn't know.

But she was still just in shock that he was here.

He closed the distance to her and swept her up over his shoulder. "Laugh all you want, wench. But you're mine."

The heat in his voice turned her on instantly.

"That's right. Your scent. Your body. Your unbelievably beautiful personality, they're all mine."

"Geesh, get a room, you two," Wilson grumbled.

Sebastien turned to glare at him with Kim still over her

shoulder. "Hush, Scallawag, before I make you walk the plank."

Wilson rolled his eyes as Sebastien hauled her down into his arms and stepped toward the edge of the railing.

Kim gave wilson a grateful look and he winked at her. Then she realized she was getting awfully close to the railing. "Sebastien, you wouldn't."

"Don't make me tie you, wench," he said, swinging her back and then toward the railing.

"Wait just a minute, now, you—oof!" Before she could make more of a protest, she found herself launched into the air. This was the second time she'd fallen off a boat, and both time had been around him.

But the water was softer this time when it broke her fall, and a splash beside her as she rose to the surface told her Sebastien had jumped in as well. He put out his arm for her and she took it and let him pull her to his boat. He helped her onto the swim platform and then into the boat.

"Thanks, Wilson," he said darkly, waving to the other man.

She wrung out her dress as she sat dripping wet in his boat. "You didn't have to get me soaked," she grumbled.

"That's punishment for leaving with another man, mate."

Her heart leapt. He'd called her mate. Out loud for the first time between them, the word had never sounded so sweet. He untied the boat and started the engine, and then pulled away.

She watched her captain drive, wondering just where he intended to take her.

***

Sebastien felt utterly stupid in the costume, but he wasn't going to let that stop him. He'd seen the sparkle in Kim's eyes when he'd pulled up to rescue, er, kidnap her, and it had been worth all the humiliation of wearing this outfit.

When he pulled up to the dock, he took her in his arms again. He didn't care who saw him carrying her. Her warmth was familiar and steadying, and he was going to make her his if it killed him.

And just let anyone try to take her away from him. Not a hundred men could do it. Not a thousand, he told himself as he stomped through the sand and toward the building that housed his suite.

They acquired some interesting looks as he walked with her through the lobby and into the elevator. It wasn't every day you saw a pirate carrying a woman up to his suite.

But she was his now and he was going to make sure she knew he'd never leave her.

Right after he heard her explanation for leaving with Wilson. He glared darkly at the elevator doors as they went up in silence.

When they arrived at his floor he walked out with her in his arms. She was quiet until they reached his suite and he deposited her in front of it to unlock his door.

"Sebastien?" she asked. "Are you angry?"

"No," he lied. He was. He'd seen her standing there with Wilson and his blood had boiled like lobster over a fire. He led her in and shut the door behind him. Then he took his hat off and tossed it aside.

She started to protest and he gave her a dark glare. "Well, it was good while it lasted," she said.

He sat on the edge of a couch and waited. "So, you didn't even give me a chance to think on things? You just went off with another male?"

"You didn't want me," she said, and he could see the hurt in her eyes.

"When did I ever say that?" he asked, astonished.

"You didn't say anything when I asked if you'd give us a chance if I was willing to go against my family."

He frowned. How had she taken that so wrong? "I didn't say anything because I was thinking. It took me some time to adjust. From the moment we started, I was telling myself that it was going to end. When I thought there was a chance you wouldn't want it to, I had to figure out what I wanted to do."

She frowned. Uh oh.

"But I knew from the moment I saw you. My bear knew. My body knew. It took a while for my mind to catch up." He walked to her and ran his hands slowly up and down her arms, soothing her and letting himself know that she was okay and here with him. "You gave me adventures and opened me up. Even if the animal inside me wasn't screaming that I was your mate, I'd want to be with you. You're the perfect match for me, Kim. And if you'll let me be your mate, I'll make sure you have a never-ending supply of adventures."

She just stared at him, eyes looking sort of watery. He reached up to brush a tear away before it could fall.

"I'll call your father. Tell him our bloodline. If it's just pure alpha he's concerned about, then it should be fine."

"He also wanted to keep his word to the other family, but Wilson sort of solved that for us."

"He turned out to be useful," Sebastien said sardonically. "Imagine that."

She swatted his arm. "He helped us."

"I know," Sebastien said, sweeping her into his arms and carrying her toward the bedroom. He tossed her on the bed and got on with her, brushing an errant braid away from her face and staring into her fathomless silver eyes. "So what'll it be, Kim? You haven't given me an answer."

"My body gave you an answer long ago, when I stole your boat. All I've wanted was you," she said. "Still, I think I can agree on one condition."

"And that is?" he asked.

"Wear that pirate outfit in bed once in a while?" she asked.

He barked out a laugh as he shrugged out of the frilly

white shirt. "Fine. But only if you excuse me from wearing it while I mate claim you."

Her mouth opened in shock. "You're going to mate me? Now?"

"Why not?" he asked. "I want to bind you to me. I want you forever. And nothing your family can do can change that."

"I know," she said. "But as of last night, we were saying goodbye. As of two weeks ago, we didn't know each other."

"And as of two minutes ago, I told you I was going to mate claim you. And I mean what I say."

She grinned and melted into his arms on the bed. "Well, I guess I can say yes to that then. And deal with the consequences tomorrow."

For a moment, rational thought tried to interfere with the moment, but then he brushed it away. The rules dictating his life had never made him happy. Not like Kim did. He ran his fingers through her smooth braids, careful not to mess any up. He loved everything about her, her dark hair, her smooth skin, her mischievous laugh and sense of adventure. And in a few minutes, she'd be all his.

He'd make it worth her while.

***

Kim groaned as Sebastien pulled off her dress and then went to work on her swimsuit top. His fingers grazing her were sheer torture, and she just wanted to rip off all of their clothing and mash their bodies together and make this thing between them permanent.

But her man was a big fan of foreplay, and she guessed she couldn't complain. Even if she was wet and ready to take him inside her right freaking now.

She growled as he played with the waistband to her swimsuit bottoms. The bed was soft beneath her and she just wanted to feel him pounding her into it. Her soft body was made to accommodate him.

"Impatient today?" he asked, giving her a calm glare that only made him look more handsome and made her feel more frustrated.

"Don't piss me off," she said. "The bear in me has been needing this from the moment I saw you in that pirate outfit."

"Don't lie," he said commandingly as he leaned forward to

nip her ear. "You've been waiting much longer."

She nodded against him as he teased the shell of her ear. He slipped a finger into her swimsuit to stroke her gently and then looked at her with wide, burning blue eyes.

"Damn, you are ready."

"Told you, captain."

"Sebastien," he said. "Right now I'm not captain. I'm not a pirate or a first mate. I just want to be *your* mate."

"Where are we going to live?" she asked.

He sat up slightly, like he hadn't considered it. "I thought you'd probably want to live here, at least until things calm down with your family. But if you want to live elsewhere, I'll go with you. Just promise you won't ever leave without giving me a chance to make you stay."

"You'll never have to make me, because I'll always want to stay," she said, stroking his hair softly. Then she grabbed a handful and wound it around her hand, pulling him in and enjoying the surprise in his gorgeous eyes and the slight twitch of muscle in his jaw. "Now give me what I want before I *take* it, captain."

His mouth widened into a grin and he had her swimsuit

off in seconds. Then he was naked and climbing on top of her. Her body was ready and waiting. She was already anticipating the delicious feel of him.

He was wearing no protection, another sign of what was going to happen between them. When two shifters mated to claim one another, they wore no protection. It could result in cubs, but it was also just what put their animals the closest. She felt the bear inside her roar in anticipation, and then he slid smoothly inside her.

He cursed and said her name. She looked over his face. His straight nose, gorgeous blond hair, pretty blue eyes. Hard, muscled body. He was stern, trying to regain control as he settled inside her. She felt his velvet hardness filling every inch of her, and she felt so at home with nothing between them. She reached up to brush his hair out of his face.

Even with him not moving, she could feel pressure building inside her. Just the way he filled her hit her just right.

Was this beautiful, stubborn man really hers? Though they'd only known each other a short time, she felt she had suffered enough to earn him.

But she knew that one could never really earn that kind of love, even if one was willing to.

He looked into her eyes as he began to move, and she closed hers as sensation started to overwhelm her. She felt like she was at the center of a swirling snowstorm, and she guessed it had something to do with his bear being close to the surface.

She could see their bears together, crossing frozen water, or rolling by a stream. She could see little cubs. She could see them as humans, together on his boat, watching every sunset. Every part of her body responded to these visions, and she felt the pressure in her rising higher with each stroke of his body against hers.

She heard words of love from him in her ear, but she could barely pay attention as the sensation inside her rose to a fever pitch. She clenched her hands into fists and curled her toes, and still the build went on.

Sebastien's breathing was rapid, hoarse. "Sweetheart," he said. "Come with me."

She wanted to, but she was almost afraid of what was on the other side. It felt so intense that she could nearly die from it. But she held on to him, digging her nails into his back as he drove again into her, this time bringing a hand up to gently press against her as he moved.

That was it. She went over the crest with a scream of his

name and a roar of her bear, and as pleasure waved through her, she felt him join her.

He uttered her name in a harsh curse and she held him as he shook against her. His hard, muscled body was completely overtaken by the sensation, and she loved watching the look on his face through the blur of her own passion.

When he finally slumped on top of her, she felt warm and sated.

"I wanted it to last longer for you," he said. "I wanted to make you go over and over." He kissed her, long and deep, and she stayed silent but met his tongue with soft caresses of her own. When he pulled back, breathing heavily, she saw shock in those stern blue eyes. "I knew it was heaven being with you, Kim. But that was out of this world."

She hugged him against her. "I know," she said. "I want to do it again."

"Only if you tell me you love me," he grumped, stroking her face.

She laughed. "I think that can be arranged."

He leaned over her, pinning her hands. "Say it," he said, leaning forward so their lips were nearly touching.

She pouted, then gave him what he wanted. "I love you. You already knew that."

"I know," he said smugly.

"Now, do I get what I want?" she asked, still pouting.

He thought about it for a moment. "Aye wench. I'll plunder that booty."

She laughed and swatted at him and then rolled together in the sheets until she ended up on top of him and they were both breathing heavily. "All right," she said. "Now hoist that mainsail."

He grinned like a true pirate.

EPILOGUE

Sebastien looked over at Kim as they drove. She was as beautiful as the day he'd met her, several months ago, and today was a special day for them.

Kim's parents had finally gotten over the shock of the broken arrangement with Wilson's family, and they were coming out here to meet Sebastien and reconcile with Kim.

His mate was playing absentmindedly with a braid. She wasn't the type to usually be nervous so he felt the need to immediately soothe her. He put a hand to her neck and played softly with the skin there and she sighed against him.

"Happy three months," he said.

She raised an eyebrow at him. "Surprised you remember. You've been so busy lately."

"Like you haven't been right there with me," he teased, thinking of all the time they'd spent on boats together. She'd been quick to learn, and though she liked to whine at times, he knew she treasured working together as much as he did.

"I don't know," she said playfully. "Going on tour boats is more fun than running them." But she gave him a sparkling grin.

"Do you miss doing law?" he asked, feeling nervous as he asked it.

She shook her head a little too quickly, then considered it. "Maybe sometimes. I guess I like rules a little more than I thought. There are some considerations though," she said, putting a hand over her stomach.

Sebastien grinned. She was at 12 weeks, so the baby books said it was finally safe to tell others about their good news. Like his father, he'd turned out to be fairly virile and it was hard not to beam with pride about it these days.

She looked beautiful. She wasn't really showing, but she was glowing and beautiful. She hadn't had bad morning sickness luckily.

"You know, if you miss law, you could still figure out what it would take to practice it here, you know, on the island."

She rubbed her abdomen absentmindedly. "I might have to anyway. Might not be able to work the boat with you. I'll miss being with you."

He parked the car in short term parking because they were a few minutes and her parents hadn't landed yet. "Look. I love you more than the ocean. If you want me to figure out how to be your documents manager while you can't come out on the ship with me, just say the word. No, actually, no words needed. I'm turning things over to Bart and Hans. They are both fully capable."

"You'd really give up going on the ship for me?" she asked.

He put a hand at her waist, looking down at her in wonder. "Yes. Of course. I love you more than anything in the world."

"I can't see you being anyone's assistant," she said, giggling as he gently moved her hair back and kissed her neck and then her ear softly. Then she sighed and relaxed against the seat. He took a quick look around to make sure no one was watching. He had ten minutes to relax and pleasure his mate and soothe her nerves away and he intended to take advantage of every second of it.

She sighed as he kissed the stress away, kissing her cheek,

her temple, her forehead, gently holding his lips to her soft skin. Then his hands cupped her face and he found her mouth, delving gently with his tongue, revealing in his ownership of her and her ownership of him.

Heat and tension rose in him as he kissed her, along with a sense of tenderness that he felt only for her. Had only ever felt for her.

"Sebastien?" she said breathlessly, holding a hand out to brush his hair out of his face.

"Yes, love?"

"I think I'm going to need you to wear the pirate outfit tonight," she said, biting her lip playfully. "It's going to be a stressful day. Seeing my parents...I don't know how I feel about that."

He frowned, wanting to protect her from everything that could make her feel scared or uncertain, but knowing that her family wasn't something he could just push away. "I'll do anything you want me to," he said. "If it'll make you laugh."

"What if they're angry?"

"When I spoke to them on the phone they seemed pretty satisfied with the arrangement," he said. "But just so you know, I won't let anyone belittle you or make you feel bad."

"You'd yell at them?"

"No, I'd just whisk you away until they were ready to behave. You're my mate. Protecting you is my number one prerogative."

She grinned. "I like that about you."

"Thanks," he said, leaning in to kiss her again. He was sinking into the warm, soft kiss, letting it heat both of them up, when he heard the loud announcement of her parent's flight.

Game time.

He sat up with a sigh and she did too. He liked the look of her, lips full and face flushed beautifully from being kissed thoroughly. He could hardly wait to get through today with her and get her alone.

He'd wear or do whatever she wanted tonight, to soothe away the stress of the day.

Tilting his head to look at her as she straightened herself up, it occurred to him that maybe she was the real pirate after all.

After all, she'd commandeered his boat and then

commandeered his heart.

And he didn't mind at all.

The End

TERRY BOLRYDER

ABOUT THE AUTHOR

Terry Bolryder enjoys writing shameless paranormal romance and reading shameless paranormal romance. And that's about all. She can be reached online at terrybolryder.com

Printed in Great Britain
by Amazon.co.uk, Ltd.,
Marston Gate.